WAYWARD WINDS OF A PROFESSION

NORMAN HALL

WAYWARD WINDS OF A PROFESSION

NORMAN HALL

ReadersMagnet, LLC

Wayward Winds of a Profession
Copyright © 2021 by Norman Hall

Published in the United States of America
ISBN Paperback: 978-1-956780-88-8
ISBN eBook: 978-1-956780-87-1

All rights reserved. No part of this publication may be reproduced, stored in a retrieval system or transmitted in any way by any means, electronic, mechanical, photocopy, recording or otherwise without the prior permission of the author except as provided by USA copyright law.

Scriptures marked KJV are taken from *King James Version* (KJV): *King James Version*, public domain.

The opinions expressed by the author are not necessarily those of ReadersMagnet, LLC.

ReadersMagnet, LLC
10620 Treena Street, Suite 230 | San Diego, California, 92131 USA
1.619. 354. 2643 | www.readersmagnet.com

Book design copyright © 2021 by ReadersMagnet, LLC. All rights reserved.
Cover design by Ericka Obando
Interior design by Dindo Sanguenza

DEDICATED TO

Our Two Sons

SKIP and **CHARLIE HALL**

Y'all were nothing but a pleasure as we guided you from childhood to adulthood.

Your mother and I thought raising you was a labor of love.

READERS—PLEASE TAKE NOTE—
THE NAMES OF THE INDIVIDUALS
PORTRAYED IN THIS PUBLICATION
AS WELL AS THE SITE LOCATIONS
HAVE BEEN CHANGED TO PROTECT

THE GUILTY

PUBLICATION BASED ON THE FOLLOWING SOURCES OF INFORMATION:

1. INTERVIEWS

2. PAST BOARD MINUTES

3. NEWSPAPER FILES

4. FILMS OF PREVIOUS GAMES

5. AUTHOR'S SUPPOSITIONS AND CONCLUSIONS

WAYWARD WINDS OF A PROFESSION
INDIVIDUALS REFERRED TO IN THE STORY
UNIVERSITY OFFICIALS

UNIVERSITY PRESIDENT .... DR. DONALD BOWEN
DEAN OF STUDENTS .... DR. WOODROW YOUNG
UNIVERSITY ATTORNEY .... MARK WOODS

BOARD OF REGENTS

CHAIRMAN OF THE BOARD .... LEE PEEBLES
VICE CHAIRMAN .... SAM SPURLOCK
SECRETARY .... CLIFF HERNANDEZ
RECORDER .... JEFF MCCORCLE
MEMBER .... TED FORD
MEMBER .... JOHNNY WATSON
MEMBER .... J.L. WILLIAMS
MEMBER .... EARL LEVY

COACHING STAFF

ATHLETIC DIRECTOR .... LEO SIMS
HEAD COACH .... WILL HAVENS
FIRST ASSISTANT .... ROBERT GILMORE
DEFENSIVE COORDINATOR .... LOYD DOGETT
OFFENSIVE COORDINATOR .... JACK ARNOLD
LINE COACH .... JIM CARSON
PASSING COACH .... JOSH LEVY
TEAM DOCTOR .... DR. SETH BURROW

FOOTBALL SQUAD PLAYERS

FIRST TEAM QUARTERBACK .... JEFF GRAY
SECOND TEAM QUARTERBACK ... DICK PARKER
THIRD TEAM QUARTERBACK .... EMMITT WILSON
WIDE RECEIVER .... ELLIS FRY
DEFENSIVE LINEMAN .... JASON FORD
DEFENSIVE LINEMAN .... JIMMY CLARK
DEFENSIVE BACK .... SHERWOOD DANIELS
WIDE RECEIVER .... JIM MAJORS MOBLEY
STUDENT MANAGER .... JAY LEVY

HOSPITAL STAFF

NEUROLOGY SURGEON .... DR. JIM COWAN
ORTHOPEDIC SURGEON .... DR. GERALD KNIGHT
MEDICAL CONSULTANT .... DR. WILLIAM ALLBRIGHT

STAR INVESTIGATIVE SERVICES

PRESIDENT .... REX OVERTON
VICE PRESIDENT .... JOHN ODOM
SECRETARY .... MIKE BARRY

NEWS MEDIA PERSONNEL

LOCAL REPORTER .... JOHN MASSEY
BLRN TV .... TOM NEALY
NATIONAL NEWS SERVICE .... HERB GORMLEY

OTHERS

COACH HAVENS' ATTORNEY .... WALTER DUNCAN

THE COACHING STAFF OF BLUEFIELD UNIVERSITY

ATHLETIC DIRECTOR, LEO SIMS

Leo Sims is in his seventh year as athletic director of Bluefield University. He came to Bluefield University after serving as assistant athletic director at Northern Waters University for four years. His background in coaching includes three successful years as head coach at Louisiana Tech and two years as assistant coach at A&I College in Corpus Christi, Texas. He also served as a student assistant coach at Arizona State where he had graduated after playing three years at a varsity assignment.

HEAD COACH, WILL HAVENS

Will Havens is in his fourth year as head coach at Bluefield University. He came to Bluefield from Mississippi Tech. Before assuming the position at Bluefield, he had spent four years as an assistant at Arkansas State followed by two years as head coach at Southwestern University.

FIRST ASSISTANT, ROBERT GILMORE

Robert Gilmore is a holdover from the previous coaching staff. Coach Havens had selected him as the line coach for his incoming staff. However, after two years, he was promoted to first assistant. Before coming to Bluefield, he had spent three years as an assistant line coach at Missouri State.

DEFENSIVE COORDINATOR, LLOYD DOGETT

Lloyd Dogett had been a coach on Havens' staff at Mississippi Tech and was selected as the defensive coordinator for the incoming staff at Bluefield. Coach Dogett had previously served at New Mexico State and at Kansas State.

DEFENSIVE COORDINATOR, JACK ARNOLD

Jack Arnold came to Bluefield fresh out of Texas Tech with an outstanding record as a running back during two very successful seasons at Tech.

LINE COACH, JIM CARSON

Jim Carson was a retired head coach who had twenty-two years of successful coaching. Coach Havens was familiar with his ability and record and convinced him to come out of retirement and back into coaching.

SECONDARY COACH, MARVIN BAY

Marvin Bay was a graduate of Bluefield High School and Bluefield University. However, his talents were displayed on the track team, winning a number of track events during his tenure at Bluefield. Because of his speed, coach Havens had plans of developing a secondary with outstanding speed.

BACKFIELD COACH, JIM DANIELS

Jim Daniels was also a holdover from the previous coaching staff. He had coaching experience which included tenure at SMA as well as Baylor University.

PASSING COACH, JOSH LEVY

Josh Levy had been an assistant at TCU during the years they had produced outstanding passing teams. He is well-respected for his ability and success in designing pass patterns as well as pass defensive strategy. He had two very successful playing years as a quarterback at LSU.

THE COACHING STAFF

The coaching staff put together by Head Coach Havens was well accepted by the university faculty, the student body, the alumni, and the fans of the athletic department. They made their presence known by visiting with the four high school coaching staffs, by visiting team practice sessions, and by attending home games when their schedules would allow. They were active in churches of their choice and accepted committee appointments in chamber of commerce activities.

They were also active in helping the counseling staff to secure college scholarships for interested students. Even after students graduated, it was not uncommon for them to return to the athletic department to visit with the coaching staff. The athletic department created and enjoyed a wholesome environment.

The multitude who require to be led still hate their leader.

William Hazlitt

WAYWARD WINDS OF A PROFESSION

CONTENTS BY CHAPTERS

BASIS FOR PUBLICATION vii

INDIVIDUALS REFERRED TO viii

    UNIVERSITY OFFICIALS
    BOARD OF REGENTS MEMBERS
    COACHING STAFF
    FOOTBALL SQUAD
    HOSPITAL PERSONNEL
    STAR INVESTIGATIVE SERVICE

CHAPTER ONE 1

    THE FIRST INJURY
    AT THE HOSPITAL
    DOCTORS' DIAGNOSIS
    PRESIDENT'S CONCERN

CHAPTER TWO 10

    THE PRESIDENT'S MEETING
    BACKGROUND OF INJURED PLAYER
    SIX-MAN FOOTBALL MANUAL
    THE SPARTA HIGH SCHOOL
    TEAM'S SUCCESS

CHAPTER THREE 43
  WITH NO SCHOLARSHIP
  DEFENSE POSITION ASSIGNMENT
  THE POSITION CHART
  THE "OUTLAW" PRACTICES
  BLUEFIELD'S SEASON BEGINS
  THE 100-YARD PASS
  THE NATIONAL NEWS SERVICE

CHAPTER FOUR 66
  WILSON'S CONDITION
  SOURCE OF BLEEDING
  COACH HAVENS
  GORMLEY'S SPORTS COLUMN

CHAPTER FIVE 93
  THE STAR INVESTIGATIVE SERVICE REPORT
  REACTION TO THE REPORT
  COMMENTS ON SIX-MAN FOOTBALL
  AN ANONYMOUS EMAIL
  UIL / NCAA SIX-MAN FOOTBALL RULES
    COMPARISON
  HERB GORMLEY'S SPORTS COLUMN

CHAPTER SIX 124
  WILSON'S CONDITION
  DISCUSSION OF THE FIRST
  ANONYMOUS EMAIL
  A SECOND ANONYMOUS EMAIL
  FALSE OBSERVER ASSUMPTIONS

THE SOURCE OF THE DEPOSITS
THE SECOND 100-YARD PASS

CHAPTER SEVEN 156

ANOTHER MEETING WITH
THE BOARD AND HAVENS
THE THIRD 100-YARD PASS
STUDENT INVOLVEMENT
A PROPOSAL FROM A PROFESSIONAL TEAM

CHAPTER EIGHT 168

GAME PREPARATION
FOR COMANCHE GAP
THE SCRIMMAGE
THE SECOND INJURY
EIGHTH GAME OF THE SEASON
GORMLEY'S SPORTS COLUMN

CHAPTER NINE 182

BOARD'S DISCUSSION WITH
COACH HAVENS
BOARD'S LIST OF CONCERNS
A DISCUSSION WITH THE BOARD'S ATTORNEY
MEETING WITH COACH HAVENS
DR. ALBRIGHT'S REPORT
ON WILSON'S CONDITION
GORMLEY'S SPORTS COLUMN

CHAPTER TEN 204
   INTRODUCTION OF COACH HAVENS' ATTORNEY
   ADMINISTRATIVE PLANNING
   HAVENS AND HIS ATTORNEY
   GAME NUMBER TEN
   HAVENS' ATTORNEY MEETS WITH SELECT GROUP
   MEETING OF THE COACHING STAFF

CHAPTER ELEVEN 226
   WILSON'S RELEASE FROM THE HOSPITAL
   MEETING OF THE ATTORNEYS
   PERSONNEL ACTION
   HAVENS' TERMINATION
   HERB GORMLEY'S SPORTS COLUMN

CHAPTER TWELVE 240
   DR. COWAN'S MEETING WITH EMMITT AND HIS PARENTS
   DR. COWAN'S MEETING WITH EMMITT
   DR. COWAN'S DISCUSSION WITH THE COACHING STAFF
   DR. BOWEN AND THE ATHLETIC DIRECTOR

CHAPTER THIRTEEN 251
   DETAILS CONCERNING AN ADMINISTRATIVE HEARING
   THE HEARING PROCESS
   EMMITT'S SECOND VISIT

TO THE PRACTICE FIELD

THE ADMINISTRATIVE REMEDY HEARING

FOLLOW-UP FROM THE HEARING

CHAPTER FOURTEEN 269

ADMINISTRATIVE PROCEDURES SET IN MOTION

EMMETT'S THIRD VISIT TO THE PRACTICE FIELD

TWO NEWS RELEASES BY BLUEFIELD UNIVERSITY

THE INTERNMENT

HERB GORMLEY'S SPORTS COLUMN

CHAPTER ONE

WAYWARD WINDS OF A PROFESSION

CHAPTER ONE

1. The First Injury

2. At the Hospital

3. Doctors' Diagnosis

4. President's Concern

WAYWARD WINDS
OF A PROFESSION

The Regional Hospital was located on Fairmont Avenue and was normally a place of quiet but steady activities. However, this was late Wednesday afternoon; an injury had occurred at the University football practice field which caused increased activity and concern.

Emmitt Wilson had been injured, and the team doctor had been called. The doctor had come to the field, and after a brief examination there, he immediately directed that the player be sent to the local medical clinic from which he was then transferred—this time to the Regional Hospital. The staff was waiting for Wilson when the ambulance arrived, and he was immediately taken to the laboratory in the emergency wing.

Dr. Burrow had called ahead to alert the two specialists to be on call for a conference concerning Wilson. As the two arrived, they were briefed as to Wilson's injury and how it had happened. After a brief examination followed by a consultation among the three doctors, it was determined that extensive x-rays needed to be made. After these, it was determined that Wilson would be assigned to a room with a 24-hour shift of nurses assigned to him.

Head Coach Havens and Athletic Director Leo Sims arrived at the hospital to inquire about Wilson's condition. They were briefed about the x-rays and some of the doctors' major concerns.

At this point, Wilson had given no indication of regaining consciousness. Athletic Director Leo Sims called Wilson's parents to inform them of their son's injury and the details of what had caused it. He gave them directions to the hospital and Wilson's room number.

Coach Havens commented, "I don't believe such a serious injury could occur as the result of a team practice. Besides, Wilson isn't even a first- or second-team player."

Dr. Cowan stated, "Coach, I don't believe you have seen that lifeless body with no movement whatsoever and an expressionless face. If you had, I do not believe you could make such a statement. This is a very serious situation, and that boy's life is hanging in the balance."

Coach Havens replied, "It's just hard for me to imagine."

Both doctors Cowan and Knight observed Wilson twice during the night, and Dr. Burrow spent much of the night going in and out to check on any response from Wilson. But the morning came with no noticeable change in Wilson's condition, and concern continued to deepen in everyone.

The next day, a 10:00 a.m. meeting of the doctors, university officials, and the coaching staff took place.

President Dr. Bowen—"Gentlemen, we have a very serious situation at hand. It has been almost 19 hours since Wilson was hurt, and he has not regained consciousness at this time. Dr. Cowan, could you please comment on this situation? Isn't it unusual for a person to be unconscious for an extended period of time like this?"

Dr. Cowan—"Yes, it is. It indicates some type of brain injury—likely bleeding in or near the brain."

President Dr. Bowen—"Are we doing everything we can to relieve the situation?"

Dr. Cowan—"No, we are not because we don't know what to do until we are able to pinpoint the location of the bleeding. Our exams have shown the massive bleeding but not the exact source. Our examination leads us to believe that he was hit on both sides of the head at almost the exact same time which has had a very damaging effect on his skull. The blow was so severe that the helmet only added to the severity of the blow."

Coach Havens—"Gentlemen, I cannot believe this situation has had the devastating effect which you are describing."

Dr. Knight—"Coach Havens, you keep trying to downplay the seriousness of this emergency. Rather than making excuses for what has happened, I suggest you turn your attention to trying to help the situation. Your actions indicate you have priorities other than the boy's health."

Dr. Cowan—"I disagree with you, coach. The injuries—notice the plural of the word injuries—were quite serious, and I doubt that this athlete will ever play another down of football."

The university members were all shocked and in disbelief.

Dr. Cowan—"This was a severe head injury as well as shoulder and neck injuries. The player had been hurt at approximately 3:10 p.m. on Wednesday. It is now 10:00 a.m. on Thursday, and he still has not regained consciousness."

After another examination of the injured player later that same day, Dr. Cowan expressed concern over the bruises and swelling on each side of the temples. As time had passed since the injury occurred, the swelling had become tinted with what seemed to be small blood pockets which were probably caused by internal bleeding which caused additional concern beyond that about his original diagnosis.

Dr. Gerald Knight, the orthopedic surgeon, expressed a new concern about the condition of the shoulder and neck injuries. Upon his first examination, he determined that the blow causing the injury seemed to have been from the side. However, after a period of time, the injury now appeared to be caused by a direct blow on top of the shoulder. The swelling, coloration, and bruising now indicated a more extended area of damage. However, no broken bones were apparent.

University President Dr. Bowen commented, "I did not think a team practicing against itself would be played with that much intensity."

One of the coaches commented that this practice session had been designed to 'get the passer.'"

President Dr. Bowen—"Get the passer" yes! But the extent to which this event took place is highly questionable. Besides, I have been under the impression that during practice sessions of this nature, the quarterback wore a red identification of some kind to prominently identify him."

Gilmore—"Yes, sir. That is normally done to protect the quarterback. I think the concern of facing a talented passer may have overshadowed our judgment this time."

President Dr. Bowen—"Who is responsible for seeing that this precaution takes place?"

Gilmore—"Sir, I suppose it is the responsibility of the entire coaching staff."

Dr. Cowan—"The head injury has all the indication of targeting."

President Dr. Bowen—"You mean to say you practice against each other with the assigned task to 'take out' a member of the opposing practice team?"

Coach Havens quickly interjects—"We do not mean to injure anyone."

Dr. Cowan—"It would seem to me that 'taking out' someone would require some type of injury, though surely not meant to be this severe."

President Dr. Bowen—"I am concerned with the boy's health and safety and am upset at the implications that this situation has brought to light. The University Board of Regents will certainly expect a detailed investigation of this matter. I expect the directed University personnel as well as the designated members of the coaching staff to be present in the executive conference room at 10:00 a.m. tomorrow morning."

As the meeting progressed, President Dr. Bowen announced that an extensive investigation would be conducted by the Star Investigative Service. All parties would be expected to cooperate fully.

There is no road like the road back home.

> Tom Goodnight

CHAPTER TWO

WAYWARD WINDS OF A PROFESSION

CHAPTER TWO

1. The President's Meeting

2. Background of Injured Player

3. Six-man Football

4. UIL / NCAA Six-man Football Rules Comparison

5. The Sparta High School Team's Success

WAYWARD WINDS
OF A PROFESSION

The President's called meeting was assembled as scheduled in the Executive Conference Room at 10:00 a.m. on Thursday. October 29, XXXX.

Dr. Bowen announced that an investigation had been scheduled to be conducted by the Star Investigative Services. As previously requested, all parties involved would be expected to cooperate fully.

The Star Investigative Service was a well-established and well-respected firm which had been in existence for over twelve years and had performed services throughout the southern part of the United States for universities, colleges, and high schools. Its staff included retired FBI personnel as well as experienced investigative individuals from the University Interscholastic League and the Association of

Sports Officials. A timeline had been placed for the due date of the report.

BACKGROUND OF THE INJURED PLAYER

The injured player was Emmitt Wilson who had been designated as a third-team quarterback. He was classified as a University junior and had been a member of the team since his freshman year. Locals who knew him or knew of him began to help piece together his background information.

Emmitt was born in a rural area of Coryell County, Texas, and attended high school in Sparta, Texas. Upon entering high school, he was interested in the sports program and in playing on the football and baseball teams. He was somewhat small and lightweight and was used as a defensive back. The high school football squad consisted of only fourteen team members, and all members received extensive practice time in several positions.

The entire school population was only 156 students, with only 53 of those in high school. Though limited in the size of its student body, the community supported a complete sports program consisting of football, basketball, track, and baseball. Because of the small enrollment in the high school, the football program was limited to a six-man team.

Six-man Football

Six-man football is played on a modified playing field of 80-yards long and 40-yards wide. However, if a six-man field is not available, an eleven-man field is authorized. All players are eligible to catch a pass, even the center. It is a fast-moving sport with much running and open-field tackling. Touchdowns earn six points, and a kicked extra point earns one point; a run or pass extra point earns two points.

In addition to being a fast-moving game, it is also a high scoring game. In fact, the rule is if one team is 45 or more points ahead at the end of the first half, one additional down is played at the beginning of the second half, and then the game is called and a winner declared. Other details of the six-man game are the following:

*goal posts are 25 feet apart;

*the crossbox is 9 feet above the ground;

*the length of quarters is 10 minutes;

*the time between quarters is 2 minutes;

*the time between halves is 15 minutes;

*the offense must advance the ball 15 yards in four downs to receive a first down;

*at least 3 offensive players shall be on the line of scrimmage at the snap of the ball;

*the ball may not be handed forward to the center

through his legs;

*the ball may be handed in any direction to any player during a scrimmage down behind the neutral zone;

*all players are eligible to catch a forward pass;

*field goals count 4 points or 2 points if successful through a place or drop kick, one point if through a successful pass or run.

Emmitt's main interest was in passing the football—however, he was never called on for that phase of the game during his freshman year. He made the first team as a defensive back in spite of his size—probably because of his desire and determination. The quarterback from the year before had graduated from Sparta, and the coach was in search of another quarterback and encouraged any of the players to try out for the position. Emmitt eagerly took advantage of the opportunity. After several practice sessions, the coach selected another player who had more experience than Emmitt and who had been on the team the previous two years. Emmitt was assigned as a defensive back position which he kept for the balance of that season. The team had a winning season his freshman year, winning six of the ten-game schedule. After practice each day as well as on weekends and holidays, Emmitt was on the practice field throwing passes to anyone who would stay and work with him.

As his second year got underway, all the long hours of practicing the passing game began to pay off. Early in

Emmitt's sophomore year, the starting quarterback suffered a knee injury and was unable to play the remainder of the season. Emmitt assumed the quarterback position, and victories seemed to follow the team as the season progressed.

Emmitt's junior year was filled with success for himself and the team. They won nine of their scheduled ten games and were declared the district winner. His senior year, the team won all ten of their district games plus the district championship as well as the regional championship. Since six-man football is normally played in rural areas with little or no newspaper coverage, such players often go unnoticed with little or no fanfare. However, Emmitt's success as a passer began to draw the attention of high school coaches at the larger high schools. Their attention was confined to the discussion of his predicted success and speculation as to his effectiveness in districts with eleven-man teams as well as in college games.

Members of the Sparta team as well as the coaches were disappointed at this lack of recognition—after all, they had won the district and regional championships. However, Sparta was located in a sparsely populated area of the state made up largely of ranches of a considerable size as well as no large towns or colleges in this section of the state.

Emmitt's senior year was filled with success with his passing record beginning to be known in a wide area of the state due to increased press coverage. Members of the press seldom came to six-man games but did provide extensive coverage of the game scores and Emmitt's passing record. During the latter part of the season, two college recruiters came to scout Sparta's game and observe any prospective college recruits. The football recruiting season passed, and college recruiting reached its high point then passed without a local six-man player being awarded a scholarship to any of the colleges or universities in the state.

sixmanfootball.com

the bible of six-man football in Texas

THIS ABBREVIATED MANUAL OF SIX-MAN FOOTBALL IS CONSIDERED THE BIBLE OF SIX-MAN FOOTBALL IN TEXAS. IT PRESENTS A BRIEF HISTORY OF THE DEVELOPMENT OF THE SPORT AS WELL AS SOME DETAILS OF SIX-MAN FOOTBALL BECOMING OF AGE IN TEXAS.

Jay Williams

Sixmanfootball.com

HISTORY

I will again start posting old issues of The Huntress Report, the newsletter I started in 1994. Here's a link to the page where the issues will be posted in pdf form. LINK TO OLD NEWSLETTERS

The text was written by myself back around 2000 and appears in the book, "King Football: Greatest Moments in Texas High School Football History." I also listed a top-10 all-time six-man games in the book, which I would recommend anyone buy, but I have not been paid (as well as many of the other writers in the book) by the guy who published it.

Six-man football was invented in 1934, by a high school coach from Chester, Nebraska named Stephen Epler, who wanted to find a way for his players to have the opportunity to play the game of football. Four years later, the game made its way to the Lone Star state, as the UIL contemplated adding six-man football to the option allowed for Texas public schools.

In the first year, 1938, only 55 schools participated in six-man football. A year later, the number grew to 112 schools. At one time as many as 160 teams participated.

In the early 1940's, towns that sixty years later still play six-man football, such as Harrold, Trent, Novice, Groom and Oglesby, were playing. But also appearing on those early charts were the then tiny towns of Katy, Friendswood, Dripping Springs, Copperas Cove and Pearland. Of course, many long forgotten towns that no longer exist or have schools were represented. Towns like Darrouzeit, Oklaunion, Flat, Pecan Gap and Stuart Place fielded teams in those early seasons.

Today, as we enter the twenty-first century, a time of consolidation and migration to the city, the game of six-man football is still alive and well in Texas. In 2001, there were 102 public schools and as many as 50-60 private schools participating. By comparison, 19 teams play in New Mexico, 16 in Colorado and 15 in Montana, the only other states sanctioning state championships, *(writer's note: of course there are several teams in various states, like Nebraska and Kansas, which play six-man football that is not sanctioned by the state association.)*

The game

that started it all in Texas...or maybe not (see below). Leman Saunders, a former player at Blackwell, has found evidence that the first six-man game in Texas was actually played in 1936, as opposed to the UIL exhibition that was played in the Spring of 1938.

PRAIRIE LEA vs. MARTINDALE (Spring 1938)

Very little is known about the exhibition these two squads put on, other than it was the first six-man football game played by Texas high school teams. University Interscholastic League Director, Rodney Kidd, asked coaches at the two schools located just south of Austin to study the rules. They later played the exhibition for UIL officials, who must have been impressed, as they officially sanctioned six-man play for the fall of 1938.

A NEW HISTORY OF SIX-MAN-BY LEMAN SAUNDERS

(updated November 11, 2016)

First of all, I want to thank Leman for doing this. He has really been the driving force in updated research of six-man football in Texas. For years we have both tried to trace the roots of those games mentioned above, but have never found documented proof that the dates actually line up. Here is his update:

It has long been rumored that Prairie Lea played Martindale in an exhibition game for the Texas Interscholastic League to observe and decide if they wanted to sanction 6-man football as an official sport and this long rumored game has been called the first 6-man football game played in Texas by many sources. It has been proven that not only was this alleged game not the first in Texas, it is unlikely that this game ever happened at all.

The first recorded 6-man football game in Texas took place on September 29, 1936 in Rotan between Sylvester and Dowell; Sylvester won 14-0. These two schools teamed up with Hobbs and McCaulley to play this new game in the fall of 1936 forming their own league and playing a round robin schedule. Sylvester went 6-0 and claimed the league title. Then in 1937 Texline High School sought out other schools in their area to form a 6-man football league and Texline for sure played at least one game against Grenville, New Mexico, losing 18-0. By the early spring of 1938 many schools took interest in 6-man football and began making moves to learn the game in order to adopt the sport by the following fall. This was fueled in part by Rodney Kidd, the newly appointed Athletic Director for the Texas Interscholastic League or TIL (later named UIL) who took office in February and as early as March started out to make 6-man football an official sport in Texas. Several clinics and a few demonstration games were played around Texas in order to show the coaches just what 6-man football was; here is a brief time line of those such games:

April 22-May, 1938 -Pioneer School Activities Association (PSAA, rival to TIL) spring football district is formed and games played between Westbrook, Coahoma, Garner (Knott), Ackerly, and Courtney.

April 27, 1938 -Lockhart newspaper per article in May 5th Lockhart newspaper, Prairie Lea and other schools' officials met in San Marcos and with the help of Rodney Kidd and Roy Bedichek organized a '6-man football league' for schools in Hays and Guadalupe counties. J.D. Fulton of Prairie Lea was elected district chairman and L. J. Wehmeyer of Prairie Lea was named secretary. Article noted that a second meeting would be arranged to make a schedule of games. This would be District 3. No mention of an exhibition game being played or set up for a future date.

April 30, 1938- Pyote played Barstow in a 6-man football game at Wink, TX.

May 5, 1938- Friona played a 6-man football exhibition game at Friona between a split squad of Friona high school players. Reds beat the Whites 31-26. Friona had intentions of playing 6-man in the fall of 1938 and even formed an early district but they changed head coaches and ended up playing 11-man instead.

July 12-15, 1938- Denton's North Texas State Teacher's College hosted a coaching clinic with a demonstration game played at the end on July 15th at 7:30 pm. Clinic was put on by Jack Sisco, coach at North Texas, and Joe Allett, varsity backfield coach at Louisiana State Normal College in Natchitoches, LA. The two teams that played the game were made up of former football players for Teacher's College. 1,500 people attended the game between the Whites and Reds; the Whites won 14-6.

July 31-August 6, 1938- Texas High School Football Coaches Clinic and school was held in Lubbock, rumored to have talked about 6-man football sometime during the clinic.

August 3, 1938- A 6-man demonstration game was played at East Texas Teachers' College in Commerce. This was held at the end of a six-week summer course on the sport. Fans attended the game which featured two teams made up of 'present and former Lion football stars.' The Blue team beat the Gold team 25-13.

Research has yet to show that the mythical Prairie Lea vs. Martindale game was one of these demonstration games, with more research needed. The best evidence that they MIGHT have played is in an article from the Amarillo News Globe newspaper on Sunday June 19th which states that 'to give school officials and coaches attending the University of Texas summer school, and others over Texas, an opportunity to see 6-man football, a game between two Austin high school teams under the direction of Coach Standard Lambert of Austin and H.L. Berridge of the university's physical education department will be played here June 28.' However, research has produced no evidence a game was played at all and if so would have likely been with college students just like the other demonstration games put on at Denton and Commerce under the supervision of the TIL throughout the summer. Summer courses were also offered at the college in San Marcos as well.

What is known is that Kidd helped form District 3 that both Prairie Lea and Martindale would be in on their formation meetings. It is likely that this has been misinterpreted over time into being an actual football game being played, but there is no mention of it in the historical record anywhere which includes the 1939 Prairie Lea yearbook, Lockhart newspapers that covered this district and its formation from the start, and The Leaguer which featured a January 1939 article written by the Martindale Superintendent about starting football at his school with again no mention of the long rumored game.

Another long circulation 'fact' is that 55 schools decided to participate in 6-man football in 1938, that also is not true as over 100 Texas schools played 6-man football in 1938. There is only one known surviving official UIL document found to date which puts the number of schools at 55, but in fact some of the schools that document lists didn't field teams in 1938 and still other schools played in the district(s) instead of them. An example of this is as follows:

Document Listed: District 4 – Blue Ridge, Floyd, Merit, Princeton, Prosper, Nevada, Josephine with no notation on who the district winner was, however Merit and Prosper didn't field teams and instead Allen and Murphy did and via newspaper articles we know Allen won the district.

Revelations like this point to the existing UIL document to be a very early document, likely being printed right around the September 15th deadline for official district recognition before all the district formation paper work was received. Based on this evidence we can openly question what schools were actually officially sanctioned as well as the number of districts in the 1938 season. Newspaper accounts have the number of schools playing 6-man football in the fall of 1938 over 100 and schools that played 6-man football in 1938 that are still playing the game today,

HISTORY AND COMMENTS REGARDING SIX-MAN FOOTBALL

To: Bluefield University Board of Regents

Ref: History and Comments Regarding Six-man Football

The history of the Six-man Organization which has supervised the existence of six-man football in Texas has had a fluctuation of member schools. Some districts have outgrown the maximum membership for a six-man membership. For example, Copperas Cove was once a member, but due to the increased mission and activities at Fort Hood, now has the four A classification. Some districts together with their towns have disappeared—for example: Sparta, Brookhaven, Topsy, and The Grove. Consolidation with larger districts is the chief reason for the loss of member schools in the six-man league. However, in its better days, it served its selected communities well.

You have been advised of the history and organization of the six-man system. In order to increase your understanding of the rules of the game, a list of 6 MAN FOOTBALL EXCEPTIONS is presented for your review.

To: Bluefield University Board of Regents

Re: Six-man Football Rules Comparison

As previously stated, additional information regarding six-man football rules as compared to regular eleven-man rules is attached for your review.

This information was taken from the official Six-man Football Manual dated 2009-2010.

~ UIL/NCAA SIX-MAN FOOTBALL RULES COMPARISON ~

General: Texas Six-Man Football Rules are the same as NCAA Football Rules except for the following variations. (Note: NCAA Rule References are indicated in parenthesis).

NCAA RULE   SIX-MAN RULE VARIATION

(1-1 & 2)   1. Each team has six players. Unless necessary to use the eleven-man field, the six-man field is 80 yards by 40 yards, with the 40 yard line being the center of the field. The two inbound lines (hash marks) are 40 feet from the sidelines. There will also be marks that are measured 13 feet from the sidelines. Goal posts are 25 feet apart and the crossbar is 9 feet above the ground.

(1-1-3)   2. When one team is 45 or more points ahead at the end of the first half or if a team achieves a 45 point lead during the second half, the game is ended immediately.

(3-2)	3. Length of quarters is 10 minutes; between quarters, 2 minutes between halves, 15 minutes.
(4-1-3)	4. During a try after touchdown the ball becomes dead when Team B gains possession or it is obvious that a kick is unsuccessful.
(5-1)	5. Offense must advance 15 yards instead of 10 yards in four downs.
(6-1)	6. Unless relocated by penalty, the kicking team's restraining line on a kickoff is the 30 yard line on a six-man field and the 20 yard line for a free kick after safety. The receiving team's free kick restraining line is 15 yards from the point of kickoff. There is no requirement to have a minimum number of players on either side of the kicker.
(6-1)	7. The ball must travel 15 yards on a kickoff (or place kick/punt after a safety) or be touched by the receiving team before members of the kicking team are eligible to touch it

(6-2) 8. A free kick out of bound between the goal lines untouched inbounds by a player of Team B is a foul (A.R. 6-2-1-I-IV). PENALTY—Live-ball foul. Five yards from the previous spot or the receiving team may put the ball in play 20 yards beyond Team A's restraining line at the inbounds spot (S19).

(7-1-3) 9. Unless the ball is kicked or forward passed, it may not be advanced beyond the neutral zone until AFTER AN EXCHANGE has been made between the receiver of the snap and another player; EXCEPTION: Any player of Team A may advance a loose football after it has been touched by a Team B player. PENALTY: 5 yards plus loss of down (illegal procedure) from previous spot (S19 & S9). An exchange is completed when possession of the football is gained by a receiver of the snap, given up voluntarily or involuntarily by file receiver of the snap, and possession is regained by another player of Team A.

(7-1) 10. If the snap is muffed and a Team A player catches or recovers the ball beyond the neutral zone, he may not advance it. PENALTY: Loss of down (illegal procedure) from previous spot (S19 & S9), 5 yards from the previous spot is also assessed if the Team A player advances the ball. If a Team A player catches or recovers the muffed snap behind the neutral zone, he may legally advance it only after a legal exchange.

(7-1-3) 11. At least 3 Team A players shall be on their line of scrimmage at the snap.

(7-1-6) 12. The ball may be handed in any direction to any player during a scrimmage down behind the neutral zone. A linesman may receive a forward hand-off at any time and is not required to be 2 yards behind his line of scrimmage and does not have to face his goal prior to receiving the hand-off. EXCEPTION: The ball may not be handed forward to the snapper through his legs. PENALTY: 5 yards from previous spot and loss of down (S19 & S9).

(7-3)	13. The ball is dead when a passer catches his own pass (untouched by B), and it is ruled as an incomplete forward pass.
(7-3)	14. All players are eligible to catch a forward pass, except that a pass is ruled incomplete when caught by the passer (see preceding rule). If a forward pass is thrown to the snapper, it must travel at least one yard in flight.
(8-1)	15. Field goals count 4 points; successful try 2 points if successful through place or drop kick and 1 point if successful by pass or run. The defense may not score on a try.
(8-1)	15. Field goals count 4 points; successful try, 2 points if successful through place or drop kick and 1 point if successful by pass or run. The defense may not score on a try.
(9-1-2)	16. When a team is in an offensive or scrimmage kick formation, a defensive player may not initiate contact with the snapper until one second has elapsed after the snap.

~ APPROVED RULINGS ~

Section 1: Exchanges:

I. First down and 15 from A's 35. A10 pitches to A28 who muffs the ball. A10 picks it up and runs to A's 45. RULING: Illegal advance by A. Penalize 5 yards plus loss of down.

II. First down and 15 from A's 25. A10 pitches the ball backward. It strikes B72 and is loose on the ground. A10 picks up the ball and runs to B's 40. RULING: A's ball first down and 15 on B's 40. NOTE: by definition, when the ball strikes B72, it has been touched by Team B player.

III. A15 hands the ball to A40. While still behind the line A40 hands the ball forward to A15 who advances beyond the line for a ten yard gain. RULING: Legal advance by A15.

IV. A12 receives the snap and possesses the ball. He hands the ball forward to A60, the snapper by handing it back between his legs. A60 advances 5 yards. RULING: Illegal Advance by Team A. PENALTY: 5 yards and loss of down.

V. A15 receives the snap and hands off to A38. A38 fumbles the ball and it is picked up by A45 (1) behind the line of scrimmage; (2) beyond the line of scrimmage. A45 advances for 10 yard gain. RULING: A legal exchange has been made. A45 may advance the football in (1) & (2).

VI. A12 receives the snap and pitches the ball to A45 who muffs the pitch and is attempting to catch the ball (bobbling it) as he crosses the neutral zone. A45 then catches the ball and advances for a five yard gain. RULING: Legal advance.

VII. A's ball first down and 15 at A's 20 yard line. A8 muffs the snap. It is picked up by A25 behind the neutral zone and advanced to A's 30. RULING: Illegal advance by A. A's ball at the point of recovery. Penalize 5 yards plus loss of down from the line of scrimmage. No legal exchange has been made since A25 was the first to possess the ball after the snap and then advanced the ball beyond the neutral zone without an exchange.

VIII. A's ball second and 5 at A's 24. A13 receives the snap and fumbles the hand-off to A30. A30 recovers the fumble and hands the ball back to A13 who advances it to A's 32. RULING: A's ball first down and 15 at the 32 yard line.

IX. A10 muffs the snap from A50. The ball rolls a few yards beyond the neutral zone where A6 (1) picks up the ball and advances; or (2) falls on the ball for the recovery. RULING: (1) Illegal, 5 yards previous spot plus loss of down. Penalty marker is dropped, play continues. (2) Legal recovery, no foul, the ball is returned to the line of scrimmage, loss of down. A legal exchange has not been made prior to advancement of the ball beyond the line of scrimmage.

X. A25 receives the snap and immediately throws a backward pass to A40 who muffs the pitch. A40 scoops up the ball from the ground and advances beyond the neutral zone. RULING: Legal, a backward pass has been thrown and a legal exchange has been completed.

XI. A's ball 1st and 15 from B's 22. A10 receives the snap and attempts to hand the ball to A20. The ball is fumbled and A70 recovers at B's 19. RULING: Illegal. PENALTY: 5 yards plus loss of down. A's ball at B's 27.

XII. A's ball 4th and 1 at B's 30. A10 receives the snap and fumbles the hand-off to A22. A22 picks up the football and advances to B's 25. RULING: Ball is dead when A22 picks up the football. No advance is allowed. NCAA. Rule 4-1-3-k applies and prohibits advance. A10 may pick up the loose ball and complete an exchange for a legal advance.

Section 2: Passing

I. A15 attempts a forward pass which is batted in the air by B73. A15 catches the ball and advances it 10 yards. RULING: Legal. Ball was touched by B.

II. First and 15 yards to go for A at their 15 yard line. A9 hands the ball forward to A30. A30 runs to the left and passes the ball to A60 while still behind the line of scrimmage. RULING: Legal pass by A30.

III. A15 receives the snap and retreats 10 yards to his own 20 yard line. Due to a heavy pass rush he immediately passes the ball to A50, his snapper, who is standing on the 19 yard line. RULING: Legal pass since the ball traveled at least one yard when passed to the snapper.

IV. A8 attempts a pass at the line of scrimmage. B75 tips the ball and it is caught by A55, the snapper, at the line of scrimmage. The ball has only traveled 1/2 yard in the air. RULING: The tipping by B makes A55's reception a legal catch and A55 may advance the ball.

V. A's ball 4th and 4 at B's 22. A10 throws a pass which strikes A73 and bounces into the air. A10 catches the ball and advances 5 yards where A10 fumbles the ball. RULING: Incomplete forward pass. B's ball 1st and 10 at their 22. (Six-Man Rule variation No's 12 & 13)

Section 3: Other Plays

I. Team A lines up at the line of scrimmage with three men on the scrimmage line next to each other in a three point stance. A80 located on the right side of the snapper raises up and shifts out 7 yards. RULING: Since A80 is at the end of the line this is a legal shift.

II. Team A lines up with four men on the line of scrimmage next to each other in a three point stance. A62 who is covered up by A80 (1) raises up from his 3 point stance before the snap; or (2) receives a forward hand-off and advances 4 yards; or (3) catches a forward pass 10 yards beyond the line of scrimmage. RULING: (1) Raise start (2) & (3) Legal.

III. Team A lines up with 4 men on the scrimmage line next to each other. A88, on the end line, leaves his position and goes in motion before the snap. At the snap, he is (1) moving toward his opponents goal line; (2) moving away from his opponents goal line and 2 yards behind the line of scrimmage. RULING: (1) Illegal motion since A88 cannot be moving toward his opponents goal (2) Illegal motion by A88. He must set for one second after leaving line. A lineman may not be in motion at the snap.

IV. Team A's kickoff from their 30 yard line rolls out of bounds untouched by Team B at B's 38. RULING: B may snap the ball at their own 38, 30, or accept the penalty against A for illegal procedure.

V. B is leading 60-19. They return the 2nd half kickoff 65 yards for a touchdown. RULING: Game ends.

VI. B is leading 50-10 in the second half. B intercepts A's pass and returns it 16 yards for a touchdown. B44 dips on the run back. RULING: If A declines the penalty the game ends and there will be no try for a point.

VII. A's ball fourth down and 5 from their 20 yard line. A14 punts the ball which is blocked and goes straight up in the air. A45 catches the punt behind the line of scrimmage and advances to A's 40 yard line. RULING: Legal advance by A, first down and 15 yards to go.

VIII. Team A attempts a try from any legal point and:

(1) Team B recovers a legal fumble, picks it up and advances the ball into Team A's end zone; or

(2) Team B intercepts a fumble or forward pass and advances the ball into Team A's end zone; or

(3) Team B blocks the try, gains legal possession and advances the ball into Team A's end zone; or

(4) Team B blocks the try and A12 picks up the ball and advances into Team B's end zone.

RULING: No score, ball is dead when it is obvious that the kick is unsuccessful.

2009-2010 Football Manual

SIX-MAN FOOTBALL
GOALPOST DIMENSIONS

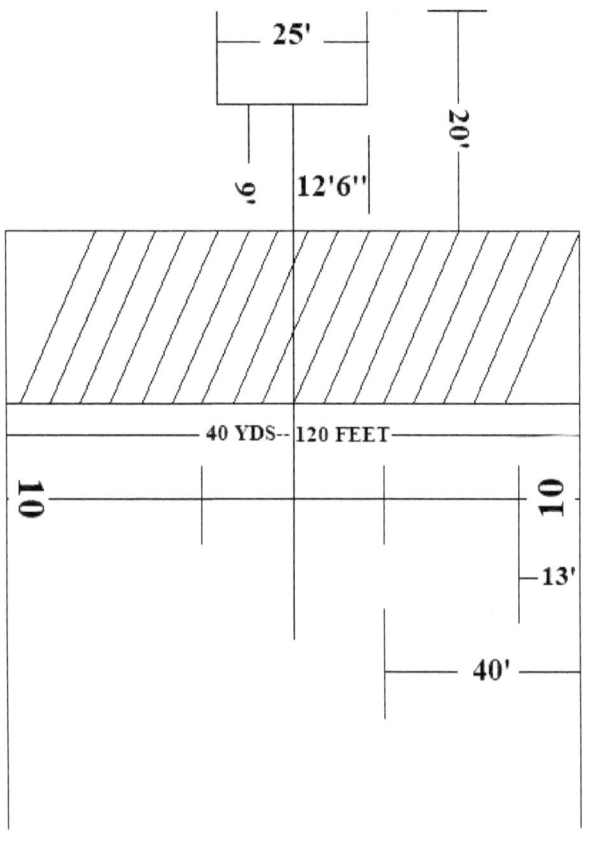

DIMENSION OF THE SIX-MAN FOOTBALL FIELD

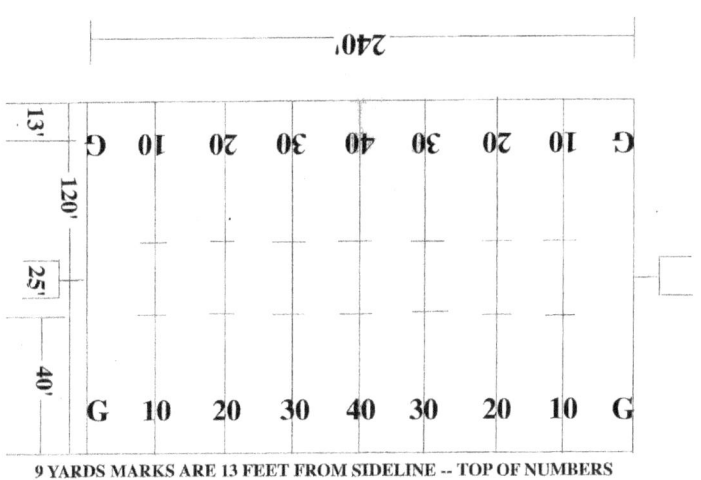

9 YARDS MARKS ARE 13 FEET FROM SIDELINE -- TOP OF NUMBERS

I have learned more from people who didn't agree with me than all the people who did agree with me.

Norman Hall

CHAPTER THREE

WAYWARD WINDS OF A PROFESSION

CHAPTER THREE

1. With No Scholarship

2. Defense Position Assignment

3. The Position Chart

4. The "Outlaw" Practices

5. Bluefield's Season Begins

6. The 100-yard Pass

7. The National News Service

WAYWARD WINDS
OF A PROFESSION

With no scholarship, on August first, Emmitt reported to the Bluefield University as a walk-on with classes scheduled to begin on September 11. Walk-ons typically receive a limited amount of attention. They were directed to observe the different phases of practice being carried out by the first and second-team designees. The emphasis of all team activity was directed at the team's preparation for the first game which was scheduled for September 3 against Tarleton State University.

Assistant coach Marvin Carson interviewed all walk-ons asking what position they had played in high school as well as preparing a list of the teams they had played against during their high school careers as well as a list of all of their team's coaches. The coach made note of the different positions each person had played. Speed and agility drills were conducted. Then the eleven walk-ons and other players not already listed on the position chart were formed into practice teams.

The position chart lists three players as to first-, second-, and third-team assignments for each offensive and defensive position. Those players not listed on the position chart were combined with the walk-ons into a practice team—or as some members of the team called it—the cannon fodder squad—which meant that this group would be sacrificed for the benefit of the learning process of the members of the first- and second-squad of the main team. As the season progressed, Emmitt played a defensive position sparingly during the ten games scheduled. Playing time was enough to give Emmitt a feel of the game and a chance to learn the defensive theories of eleven-man football that he had not been exposed to at this stage of his football development. The season went well; however, no mention was made of a scholarship or using him as a practice quarterback. The practice sessions consisted of running plays and ten- and twenty-yard pass plays.

His sophomore year started much the same as Emmitt had previously experienced. He was again assigned as a defensive back on the player position chart. This year his position entailed a detailed study of passing patterns and a defense of each of the common patterns. Emmitt welcomed this experience because he could tie it to his own experiences of passing patterns and executions. Jeff Gray continued to do well as the first team quarterback. However, his short passes allowed the defense to concentrate its manpower in a concentrated area within twenty to thirty yards of the line of scrimmage which resulted in pass interceptions being more common than desired. His accuracy and speed of delivery earned him a high completion passing score. His Eagle team continued to win their schedule of competition and receive the attention of press coverage in state and local news.

Emmitt continued to be used at his defensive back position with no exposure to the quarterback position.

THE "OUTLAW" PRACTICE

Since Emmitt had not been involved in any first-team practice sessions, he felt the need to create some activity which might improve his passing ability. To meet this need, he asked three of the other walk-ons to stay after each scheduled practice and go through some sort of a passing exercise. Several of the other walk-ons readily agreed, and each day after practice they participated in an hour or so of additional practice.

BLUEFIELD UNIVERSITY
THE EAGLES FOOTBALL SQUAD
POSITION CHART

The position chart is actually the nerve center of the football squad. It is posted on the bulletin board at the field house for all to see. It reflects the position a squad member has earned through practice and actual game experience.

Common practice for a football squad is to establish at least three teams with individuals assigned by name to offensive and defensive positions. The teams are designated as first, second, and third and are normally referred to by colors such as red, blue, and gray teams. Squad members not designated in the color designated teams are normally organized into practice teams in order for them to be involved in the overall program. Through performance on practice teams or other types of recognition, a player can earn a position on the position chart. A person assigned to a position on the blue, red, or gray team can lose his assigned position through poor performance during a game or during practice sessions—thus creating an opportunity for practice team members to advance.

The position chart presents a visual ranking as to the individual performance at each position on the color teams. Members of the news media often keep abreast of any changes in position designations which serve as a basis for news items from time to time.

BLUEFIELD UNIVERSITY
THE EAGLE FOOTBALL SQUAD

Position Chart
OFFENSIVE

SQUAD	QB	RB	FB	WR
BLUE				
RED				
GRAY				

LT	LG	CENTER	RG	RT	RE

LE

SQUAD
BLUE
RED
GRAY

Other Team Members
_____
_____
_____
_____

Walk-ons
WILSON
_____
_____
_____

Emmitt first used the passing patterns which the varsity team used in their game preparations, but as time passed, he began to extend the length of the patterns to 40- and 50-yards in length. This new length seemed to please Fry and Majors (two of the first-team receivers) as they continued to ask for the longer patterns in the workouts. The workouts were quite exhausting because of the repeated runs of 40- and 50-yards. However, Fry's comments amounted to a positive reaction by saying such workouts would keep one in physical shape. The workouts were improved a great deal when two defensive players were added in order to make the plays more realistic with the defensive player blocking the receiver as he came off the line of scrimmage and then made the pass catch more competitive as he attempted to intercept or interfere with the receiver's catch.

Emmitt's friendship with Ellis Fry, one of the starting wide receivers, continued to grow, and he continued to come to the practice field on Saturday mornings and Sunday afternoons to take part in Emmitt's passing exercises. He was especially interested now that Emmitt continued to develop his accuracy using his flip motion which increased the distance his passes traveled. Fry, as the first-squad wide receiver, took a special interest in the long passes. The importance of timing was stressed as a part of Emmitt's "outlaw" practice sessions conducted in the afternoons on Mondays, Tuesdays, and Wednesdays. Ellis had encouraged Jim Majors to start attending the practices—thus making two first team receivers participating in Emmitt's long passing patterns. Adding a stopwatch to the practice drills further enhanced the timing aspect of the practice.

Emmitt's high school coach had told him that it was important for the pass receiver to be aware of what was taking place behind the line of scrimmage as he raced down the field on their pass pattern routes. As a result, Emmitt stressed to the receiver that when the ball was snapped, the quarterback was to move from underneath the center to a position behind the line of scrimmage—once this position was arrived at—then a time must transpire as the quarterback assumes his passing stance position—then locate the receiver and launch the pass. These activities are taking place under duress and at the same time make the decision as to whether to launch the pass.

At the same time the quarterback needs to be aware that the receiver is likely being challenged as he leaves the line of scrimmage and will be forced to run his pass route in close quarters with the defensive back and then if the pass is launched the catching of the pass will be contested by the defensive back.

During the summer before his junior year, Emmitt approached the backfield coach and asked to be used as the quarterback for the practice squad. Coach Ford was unaware of Emmitt's high school experience as a quarterback and made no promise but stated that he would consider the request when planning for the coming season.

His junior year brought changes to Emmitt's position on the position chart. He was listed as the third-team quarterback. This enabled him to take part as a quarterback in some of the scrimmages scheduled each week. It seemed to Emmitt that each time Head Coach Havens did not attend a scrimmage or practice session, Offensive Coach Arnold placed him in a passing situation. However, any time Coach Havens returned, Emmitt was again placed in a background assignment.

At one time during an August practice session, Coach Arnold commented to Coach Havens that he would like to use Emmitt more in the quarterback position. Coach Havens replied, "Why do you keep pushing that character? He never played anything but six-man football in high school. He doesn't have the background to play in our system."

"I think he would surprise you, coach!" Arnold responded.

BLUEFIELD UNIVERSITY
THE EAGLE FOOTBALL SQUAD

Position Chart
OFFENSIVE

SQUAD	QB	RB	FB	WR
BLUE				
RED				
GRAY	WILSON			

	LT	LG	CENTER	RG	RT	RE

SQUAD	LE
BLUE	
RED	
GRAY	

Other Team Members _____   Walk-ons _____
_____   _____
_____   _____
_____   _____

BLUEFIELD UNIVERSITY
BLUEFIELD'S FOOTBALL SCHEDULE
XXXXX

DATE	OPPONENT	LOCATION
September 3rd	TARLETON STATE	HERE
September 10th	OKLAHOMA TECH	AWAY
September 17th	MISSOURI	HERE
September 24th	FORT LUCAS	HERE
October 1st	ALABAMA TECH	AWAY
October 8th	TULSA UNIVERSITY	AWAY
October 15th	**OPEN DATE**	
October 22nd	PERMIAN BASIN	AWAY
October 29th	COMANCHE GAP	HERE
November 5th	THE COASTAL UNIVERSITY	HERE
November 12th	COLORADO TECH	AWAY

BLUEFIELD EAGLES
THE FIRST GAME OF THE SEASON: TARLETON STATE UNIVERSITY
SEPTEMBER 3ʳᴰ

The Eagles of Bluefield University were victorious in their first game of the season. Tarleton State presented a powerful running game combined with a moderate passing attack. Three minutes and nine seconds before the half, Bluefield's quarterback had an equipment problem and had to leave the playing field. Dick Parker, the second-team quarterback, was unavailable—so Wilson was sent into the game. But only running plays were called until half-time—no pass plays were called. After the half, Jeff Gray returned as quarterback, and Emmitt stayed near the offensive coordinator Coach Arnold who received the plays called from the press box and passed them along to the Bluefield quarterback on the field. Emmitt was interested in the game plan as it unfolded with the plays called. Gray did well in directing the team in executing each play when put into action. Bluefield's combined running and passing attack scored a victory of 28 to 17.

BLUEFIELD EAGLES
THE SECOND GAME OF THE SEASON: OKLAHOMA TECH
SEPTEMBER 10TH

The second game of the season was against Oklahoma Tech which had been predicted to win the conference. The contest provided strong ground games from each team. The first half ended with a score of Oklahoma Tech 14 and Bluefield 10. During the third quarter, each team scored a touchdown. The fourth quarter consisted of strong defensive plays by both teams. Wilson was sent in during the fourth quarter with some 7 minutes and 9 seconds remaining in the game. A mixture of passes and ground plays enabled Bluefield to score a touchdown with 1 minute and 16 seconds left to play. Oklahoma Tech ran a ground-play which yielded seven yards; the next play was an incomplete pass. The third play was another ground-play. Bluefield went on offense from their own 41-yard line. The instructions from the Bluefield bench to Wilson were "Play it safe—try to run out the clock!" Bluefield was able to post another win. When he was not in the game, Wilson again stayed near Coach Arnold to observe the plays selected in relation to the team's line yard position on the field.

BLUEFIELD EAGLES
THE THIRD GAME OF THE SEASON: MISSOURI TIGERS
SEPTEMBER 17TH

During the third game of the season, Bluefield's quarterback, Jeff Gray, injured his right knee which required him to be replaced in the lineup by Dick Parker, the second-team quarterback. The score was tied at the half at 17 to 17. As the game continued, each team scored a touchdown. Late in the fourth quarter, the Tigers scored a field goal and a touchdown which gave them the lead at 34 to 27. At this point with only 3 minutes and 7 seconds left in the game, Parker was tackled hard on his own nine-yard line and had to leave the game. At that time, Head Coach Havens said to Arnold, "Go ahead and put in 'what's his name.' With us on our own nine-yard line, he can't hurt us much more."

THE 100-YARD PASS

Emmitt went in as the new quarterback. After two plays with no gain, Coach Arnold sent in a pass play. The ball was snapped to Emmitt who was rushed by the opposition but moved to the right sideline and then quickly to the left sideline. He was standing on his own goal line when he set his position to throw. Wide receiver Fry was crossing the nine-yard line of the Tigers when he caught the pass from

Emmitt and went on to cross the goal line. The hometown crowd went wild with excitement.

The Eagles kicked the extra point and then executed a successful onside kick off. Emmitt guided the Eagles down the field with four short passes to within field goal range of the Tigers' goal post. Then a successfully executed field goal brought the final score to 37 for the Eagles and 34 for the Tigers.

The local and state press coverage concentrated on the long pass play, calling it a one-hundred-yard pass. When Coach Havens was asked to comment on Emmitt's passing, he responded with, "The boy has a lot of luck. That was an outlaw play. We do not have that play in our playbook."

"Well, coach, maybe you should!" said one member of the press.

"The kid is not that good! He throws the ball, and Fry runs under it." Havens responded.

"That may be, coach, but the process certainly is effective!" replied John Massey, a sportswriter for the <u>Dallas Morning News</u>.

Another member of the press stated, "I am sure that is a true statement—but Coach Havens, the ball has to be there before Fry can run under it!"

THE NATIONAL NEWS SERVICE
SPORTS REVIEW

by

Herb Gormley

I have been involved in the adult sports world since I finished college. I was then employed as a sports reporter for a small-town newspaper covering middle school and high school sports. Over the years through tenure and experience, I moved into college and university coverage. During that time, I have made a detailed study of the game of football as well as the players who participated in the sport. This also entailed an analysis of the coaches involved in directing and supervising the game.

When I was first advised that a university player at Bluefield University had thrown what was referred to as a 100-yard pass and then an 83-yard pass in the same game, my curiosity was aroused, and I wanted to learn more about that game as well as some background of the individual performing such outstanding feats.

Upon arriving at Bluefield University to explore the details of this game involving the 100-yard pass, I was amazed to learn that the player who threw these passes was listed as a third-team quarterback and had played only a total of three minutes and seven seconds in the game. Emmitt Wilson is the player performing as quarterback for the three minutes and seven seconds. He is classified as a junior and played six- man football at Sparta High School. There seems to be a stigma attached to him because of his six-man football experience. I decided to dig further regarding his experience.

I did learn that his experience as a quarterback at Sparta High School included two years of directing the team to the district and regional championships. I also learned—which I did not know—that six-man football in Texas is limited to regional championships.

Weldon Hillard, who has been the six-man football coach at Sparta High School for nine years, has a reputation of being one of the outstanding six-man coaches in the state. A number of times he has been offered head coaching positions for eleven-man teams, but he has remained at Sparta.

On a Wednesday afternoon, Herb Gormley appeared at the high school practice field where he observed the extra practice being conducted by Emmitt Wilson with a center and two receivers. Herb had no discussion or comments during the practice session. However, as the practice drew to a close, he asked Wilson if he could visit with him regarding his passing technique. Wilson readily agreed.

Gormley—"Emmitt, I am Herb Gormley. I represent the National News Service as one of their sports reporters. I am interested in you as a player and as a person."

Wilson—"Yes, sir."

Gormley—"I am fascinated by the distance you are able to throw the ball as well as your accuracy. Where did you acquire your passing background as well as your theory of the long pass?"

Wilson—"Coach Weldon Hillard, my six-man football coach at Sparta High School, taught me all I know about passing. I may have extended the distance somewhat, but my high school coach was the source."

Gormley—"Why do you practice here at the high school field rather than at the University?"

Wilson—"In the beginning, we used the University field, but after a few sessions, we were asked to find some other place to practice. So we went to the city park for a while and finally secured permission from the high school coach to use this field when it's not in use on Mondays, Tuesdays, Wednesdays, and sometimes on Thursdays, as well as weekends and holidays."

Gormley—"Do you do anything different in your practice here that you would not do at the regular practice?"

Wilson—"Yes, we do. I am only the third-string quarterback, so my regular practice time is somewhat limited. But the long pass is pretty much based on timing."

Gormley—"Tell me more about what you mean by timing."

Wilson—"We have identified three key areas on the field that are the key to the long ball passing attacks. All three keys must fall in place for the long pass to be successful. The first area is the 30-yard line, another at the 50-yard line, and the last at approximately 70 yards down the field. These three spots will dictate the pass execution. The yard designation is important as it is the spot we analyze where the defender is located in relation to our receiver."

Gormley—"Where did this plan of execution come from?"

Wilson—"My six-man football coach, Weldon Hillard."

Gormley—"I have been involved in football playing and coaching most of my adult life, but this approach is new to me."

Wilson—"A lot of the success that we have had this season is because of receiver Fry's speed. Another factor is with these designated distances. I know where to look without having to search for a likely receiver. Without Fry's speed, some of the plays would not produce."

Gormley—"You say you know where to look before passing? What do you look for?"

Wilson—"The location of the receiver. Where is the defensive player? Is he on top of him, or is there room between our receiver and the defensive back? Is our receiver in a position to break away?"

Gormley—"No wonder you and your group practice so long and hard!"

Wilson—"Another thing you might be interested in is our time schedule for the quarterback. We compute during every practice session these three things:

1. How many seconds would lapse as the quarterback moved from under center to a passing position behind the line of scrimmage to take up a passing stance?
2. How long for the quarterback to locate an eligible receiver?
3. How many seconds for the ball to reach the receiver?

All of this will determine if we will attempt a long pass."

Wilson—"Mr. Gormley, another thing we practice here is the coverage the opposing team gives us. We realize that once a couple of our long passes are successful, the other team will increase the coverage from one to two defensive backs covering each receiver and begin to start blocking our receivers as they attempt to run their assigned passing routes and make the pass catch more competitive as he attempts to intercept or interfere with the receiver's catch. This action will influence the patterned running route of our receivers. Therefore, our passing routes must be made up of a mixture of routes all going toward the goal line. Speed is vital to our success—we must be able to outrun or out-maneuver our coverage."

Gormley—"That is quite a detailed process. You have certainly enlightened me as to your practice sessions. I thank you for this enjoyable and enlightening conversation."

Wilson—"Mr. Gormley, please understand that we are not practicing like this in defiance of the coaches. We respect them and cooperate in every way with their coaching strategy. Our purpose is to become better players, and we hope that what we do here will in time blend in with the overall football program."

It was impossible to get a conversation going; everybody was talking too much.

Yogi Berra

CHAPTER FOUR

WAYWARD WINDS OF A PROFESSION

CHAPTER FOUR

1. Wilson's Condition

2. Source of Bleeding

3. Coach Havens

4. Herb Gormley's Column

WAYWARD WINDS
OF A PROFESSION

The third day after the scrimmage in which Emmitt was injured, he was still confined to a hospital bed. Dr. Cowan was in conference with Emmitt's parents, Dr. Bowen, and the team doctor, Dr. Burrow.

Dr. Cowan—"After three days, Emmitt's condition has not improved to the extent we had hoped it would—although some progress has been made. The problem of most concern is the continuous lapse into unconsciousness. This still occurs every six hours or so but does not last so long as it had in the beginning. It now lasts some 45 minutes rather than over seven hours as it had in the past. Emmitt continues to complain of a constant headache. The positive aspect of the situation is that he has some recall of past events when he returns to consciousness. The lapse into unconsciousness is normally caused by an accumulation of blood somewhere in the brain area, but there is no supporting evidence that this is the case here. At one time, the condition seemed to indicate that a brain operation would be necessary, but we are holding off on this procedure at this time. However, in the event that the blood begins to clot, we will have no choice but to operate. We will continue our around-the-clock monitoring of Emmitt's condition and will keep you informed."

Wilson's mother—"Doctor Cowan, I understand that Wilson's problem was caused by a blow to the head—wouldn't the helmet protect against such a blow?"

Dr. Cowan—"Yes, under ordinary circumstances that would be true. A blow on only one side of the head would allow the other side of the helmet to absorb some of the force of the blow. But in this case, since there seemed to be almost equal pressure on each side of the helmet, there was no room to allow for any absorption. So the power or force of the two simultaneous blows remained in the area of the brain."

Wilson's mother—"The bleeding you speak of—is it likely coming from the area that is located around the brain, or is it coming from the brain itself?"

Dr. Cowan—"That is what we have been unable to determine at this point. Once the swelling goes down a little more, we should be able to make a determination. If the bleeding is coming from some area outside the brain, we should be able to stop the bleeding which would put us on the road to recovery."

Wilson's mother—"And if it is coming from the brain? What then?"

Dr. Cowan—"Such a situation would present a different set of circumstances as well as a challenging situation."

Wilson's mother—"Dr. Cowan, I feel you are being very kind to me and do not wish to alarm me any more than I already am—but are you really saying under such a turn of events it would present a life and death situation?"

Dr. Cowan—"Under the worst possible situation, that might be the case; however, our entire staff is pulling for Emmitt, and we will do everything in our power to bring him through this injury."

Wilson's father—"If Wilson comes out of this injury, do you think he will be able to take part in the spring practice?"

Dr. Cowan—"Mr. Wilson, it is far too early to tell at this time. We would hope so."

After asking a few more questions, Emmitt's parents departed.

Dr. Burrow—"How is Emmitt's attitude? What are his concerns at this time?"

Dr. Cowan—"He is still overwhelmed by what has happened, but it is gradually coming together. He does, however, still have questions leading up to and throughout the scrimmage. He indicated the lapses into unconsciousness come on without warning, and this is a concern to him. He also says he feels like he is rolling forward on the balls of his feet anytime he stands. He indicated that he does not want to miss spring training with the team."

Dr. Cowan now allowed team members to visit with Emmitt so long as the visits were limited to three players at a time and for only twenty minutes. The number of visits per day was to be limited to no more than three. The doctors hoped that these visits would enhance Emmitt's spirits.

Coaches and team members continued to come to the hospital to inquire about Wilson's condition. Members of the team's three different squads had divided the 24-hour day into segments with each team taking a shift so that a team member was at the hospital all day and night.

At one point, Herb Gormley approached Coach Havens and asked, "What do you think this injury will do to your chances of winning the conference?"

Coach Havens—"No effect at all—Emmitt Wilson was only a third-team quarterback."

Gormley—"ONLY! How can you say that, coach? He threw an almost 100-yard pass and almost singlehandedly won a game for you!"

Coach Havens—"Remember, Wilson has had only 6-man football experience. He is not in the same league with our other quarterbacks. Six-man football is more like kids playing running base. It is far from eleven-man football."

Gormley—"Coach Havens, your evaluation of six-man football is far different from mine. I played six-man football at Copperas Cove High School for three years on a championship team. I have a great deal of respect for six-man football. I think all players of six-man football need to be in excellent condition because every player is involved in every play."

Coach Havens turned and left the room without making additional comments.

Gormley turned to other people in the room. He approached Athletic Director Leo Sims and asked—"You said Wilson is not on a scholarship?"

Athletic Director Sims—"No, he is not on a scholarship."

Gormley—"Are his parents paying for his college expenses?"

Athletic Director Sims—"He has a student job on campus. He cleans the second floor of the chemistry building."

Gormley—"What does this job pay?"

Athletic Director Sims—"It covers his room and board."

Gormley—"How long has he had this job?"

Athletic Director Sims—"Ever since his freshman year."

Gormley—"How in the world can he do that job and meet the football practice schedule?"

Athletic Director Sims—"The lights are on in the second floor of the chemistry building and burn late into the night during football season. And some of his team members help him from time to time."

A VISIT BY THE COACH

Wilson asked if he could visit with Ellis Fry and Coach Havens. Fry came almost immediately. He greeted Emmitt warmly and expressed disappointment at the turn of events involving Emmitt's injury. He told Emmitt about the squad being divided in groups that had someone at the hospital night and day. Emmitt seemed pleased to hear of the team's concern.

Emmitt asked questions concerning the team's continued preparations for the Comanche Gap game.

Emmitt—"Fry, I have had something in the back of my mind when I have been conscious concerning Wednesday's practice."

Fry—"Ask away, and I will try to answer."

Emmitt—"I am not sure if I imagined this or if it actually happened, but during the scrimmage I thought I heard Coach Havens yell after our offensive team completed a pass of some 40 yards something like 'Take him out of there!' and then in a voice not so clear 'Hurt him!' Did that really happen?"

Fry—"I did not hear that. I had gone to the club house for a lace for my shoulder pads. But that is the talk of the team members who say they heard Coach Havens' expression concerning rushing the passer."

Emmitt—"That disappoints me—I will always remember hearing that expression!"

Fry—"Emmitt, I am sure it was an expression brought on by the excitement of the practice. Coaches have all really been concerned about the remaining games."

Emmitt—"You have answered my question, and thanks for coming by. Tell the squad 'hello' from me and thank them for their concern."

After Wilson's discussion with Ellis Fry, he asked to see Coach Havens.

Coach Havens—"Hi, Wilson. We are glad to see you are making progress and are returning to normal."

Emmitt—"Thank you for coming, Coach. I wanted to ask you some questions concerning Wednesday's practice."

Coach Havens—"Yes—certainly. What is on your mind?"

Emmitt—"Coach, this is my third year as a member of your team, and during all that time, I have never heard you call my name until you walked into this room a few minutes ago."

Coach Havens—"Oh! I can't believe that, Wilson. I may have referred to you as halfback or by your nickname, but I certainly know your name."

Emmitt—"I can't imagine why you dislike me so. I have never spoken disrespectfully to you or about you. I have always been eager to play and tried to comply with any coach's request or suggestion."

Coach Havens—"I know you have, son."

Emmitt—"Coach, please don't call me 'son.'"

Coach Havens—"All right. I meant to use it as an indication of respect."

Emmitt—"I understand your concern over the game with Comanche Gap, but during the scrimmage on Wednesday during one of the plays where the defense was charging on one of the pass plays, I heard you yell something to the effect of—'Get him out of there!' Then in a somewhat garbled voice, 'Hurt him!'"

Coach Havens—"I did not say 'Hurt him!' I was absorbed in the scrimmage and was upset by the poor showing of the defensive squad."

Emmitt—"Well, they certainly came in a big way. They did more than just take me down, and they did hurt me-just as you asked."

Coach Havens—"Oh, Wilson, I am sorry you feel that way."

Emmitt—"Well, it's over now. I appreciate your coming by."

During a session with the Board of Regents, Dr. Cowan reported on the source of Emmitt's brain bleeding.

Dr. Cowan—"The source of Emmitt's brain bleeding is a colloid cyst which is causing pressure on the brain which, as a result, is causing the brain to bleed."

Spurlock—"I believe you said earlier that this condition could be fatal?"

Dr. Cowan—"Yes, if we cannot stop the bleeding, the result could be fatal."

McCorcle—"How could such a simple scrimmage under normal conditions turn into such a monster?"

Chairman Peebles—"It has become a monster for sure! The team will be finishing its schedule of games soon. I recommend we allow Havens to finish the season before we take any disciplinary action. What is the feeling of the rest of the Board?"

Spurlock—"What do you have reference to when you say disciplinary action?"

Chairman Peebles—"A number of questionable decisions have been made by Coach Havens which I feel need an explanation."

Hernandez—"He does not deserve it, but I think that is a wise decision."

McCorcle—"But what if the team wins the conference?"

Spurlock—"They lost last week's game to Comanche Gap, and under the current circumstances, winning the next two games does not look favorable."

Chairman Peebles—"Until further developments, let's proceed as if the team will not win the conference championship."

Ford—"So, what is our next step?"

Chairman Peebles—"We will end Havens' contract, right?"

Spurlock—"Yes! Without question!"

Chairman Peebles—"He will likely ask about a buyout."

Mills—"Mr. Sims, what would a buyout cost?"

Athletic Director Sims—"A negotiated contract could cost anywhere from a full buyout which means we would pay him his full salary as if he were fulfilling the days remaining on his current contract, or if we negotiated a settlement, it could call for an abbreviated number of days which could be payment for the days remaining in the current school year or any amount of time in days, months, or years agreed upon."

Spurlock—"I don't believe we should buy him out! He does not deserve such a deal!"

Chairman Peebles—"Whatever we decide, Havens is likely to take legal action."

Mills—"Let him! He has the balance of his career to lose if he takes this public!"

Chairman Peebles—"If that happens, the next step would be the two lawyers—his and ours—meeting. In that case, we would need to inform our lawyer what we would settle for if anything less than a full resignation with no monetary payment of any kind. I will meet with our attorney and ask for guidance as to our next action."

Mills—"I have a question. What will happen to the football saff when Havens is terminated?"

Athletic Director Sims—"Their future with the University would be determined by the next head coach we employ. I would suggest we keep the staff employed for the balance of this school year. Under similar circumstances elsewhere, they would start looking for employment at other colleges and universities. Normally, the new coach would keep two or three of the old staff to help the new staff evaluate and determine position placements for the next season."

President Dr. Bowen—"I think that would be a wise move. Let's ask the Board for their approval of such action."

Athletic Director Sims—"With the kind of publicity this may generate, there is a strong possibility some team members may seek to transfer to another team elsewhere. Coaches wishing to seek employment at other institutions may find that there is a stigma attached to having been employed at Bluefield."

Ford—"I wonder how Herb Gormley will treat this development in his column?"

As chairman of the Board of Regents, Peebles met with attorney Mark Woods and President Dr. Bowen for the purpose of seeking guidance in the current situation. Woods advised the Board to meet and stipulate their specific reasons for taking action to terminate Havens' contract. Then they should meet with Havens and present the list of grievances as well as the Board's decision to terminate his contract.

At the request of the chairman of the Board of Regents, President Dr. Bowen scheduled a meeting for 2:00 p.m. the next day. The only agenda item was action concerning Coach Havens and the coaching staff. The University attorney was scheduled to attend as well as Dr. Cowan, the neurology surgeon. After calling the meeting to order, Peebles began.

Chairman Peebles—"Fellow members, we have some decisions to make regarding the future of the Athletic Department of the University."

Spurlock—"Let's list the decisions we need to make and why."

Chairman Peebles—"First and foremost, we need to determine Havens' future with the University."

Williams—"Well, first, I think we need to have the latest information concerning Wilson's progress."

Dr. Cowan—"Members, Wilson's condition has deteriorated since I last reported to you. We have detected brain bleeding in Wilson. As of yet, we are unable to determine the extent of the condition. But this is definitely a setback. This is all due to the head blows he received."

McCorcle—"Well Dr. Cowan, what does that mean for his future?"

Dr. Cowan—"The cause of the bleeding will have much to do with his future. It could be that he will never throw another pass in a scheduled game. We are searching for the cause. Please do not talk of this condition outside of this meeting, but you need to know the vast possible effects that his injury may have."

Spurlock—"Good gosh! I am stunned by this information! Is it possible that this could be fatal?"

Dr. Cowan—"It is possible if we cannot determine the cause of the bleeding."

Mills—"I am so sorry, but I cannot go on with this meeting at this time. I need time to reflect on this information and to learn more about such a condition and how it has affected Wilson."

Cloud—"This is a diagnosis that I also must have time to process. Let's adjourn for now."

At this point, Board members Mills and Cloud left the meeting room to be joined shortly by Spurlock.

Chairman Peebles—"Dr. Cowan, I don't remember ever hearing the diagnosis of 'brain bleeding' before."

Dr. Cowan—"You may not have heard it before because it is often fatal and is in junction with other causes of death. I did not mean to break up your meeting, but we need to face all possible developments. This developed only a few hours ago."

Chairman Peebles—"We understand and realize the need for such information. We will adjourn the meeting at this time."

As most of the members of the Board of Regents went in their different directions, Chairman Peebles requested a meeting with Athletic Director Sims.

Chairman Peebles—"I am concerned with the actions of Coach Havens. He is not exercising the leadership of this situation as I would have expected. He gives me the impression that he wants to keep the details of this event almost a secret. He is not facing the facts of the situation and is trying to soft-peddle the injury of Wilson as if it will go away."

Athletic Director Sims—"I have been disappointed in his attitude concerning Wilson's injury. He is not admitting the gravity of the injury."

Chairman Peebles—"Whether he intends to or not, his actions make it plain that the welfare of Wilson is not a priority of his concern."

Athletic Director Sims—"In the almost five years he has been head coach, I have never witnessed anything even similar to his dealing with personnel matters in this case."

Chairman Peebles—"Do you know of any reason for his attitude in this phase of the situation?"

Athletic Director Sims—"I feel sure he now has second thoughts about accepting the two gifts from Jeff Gray's dad. The student body is now aware of the gifts—they too are referring to them as the thirty pieces of silver—comments have been made referring to the gifts as to 'buying' the position of quarterback."

Chairman Peebles—"I am sure Mr. Gray meant well, but his action is adversely affecting the coaching staff as well as the entire team."

STUDENT INVOLVEMENT

Rumors were rampant among the student body concerning the football situation. With Wilson's passing record and his lack of playing time, the coaching staff had few supporters among the students, and even the faculty began to voice criticism toward the athletic department.

Wilson paid little heed to the criticism of the football program and purposely avoided becoming involved in any discussion of the situation. He began to receive ample help from other students with his janitorial duties in the chemistry building.

With the help of three faculty members, the student body received permission to schedule a meeting of the student body at the football stadium to discuss the actions of the coaching staff. Willson requested that the meeting **NOT** take place; however, it was scheduled to take place at 8:00 p.m. following the Comanche Gap game.

From: Chairman Peebles

To: Members of the Board of Regents

Several of our board members have brought up items included in Herb Gormley's column which have added to our discussions. Herb is a popular and respected sports reporter whose sports column appears in a number of state and local newspapers. Since he seems to have taken an interest in the Bluefield athletic situation, I feel we should be kept abreast of any of his columns relating to our Athletic Department. Therefore, any such columns will be distributed to members of the Board of Regents as we meet from time to time.

THE NATIONAL NEWS SERVICE
SPORTS REVIEW
by
HERB GORMLEY

Sports have played a big part in my life since I was in the eighth grade. I played football in middle school and then on into high school. While in high school, I played defense until my junior and senior years when I played quarterback. I loved the game and still do. Because of my infatuation with the game, I studied the original development and popularity of the sport. To me, it has a science, fascination, and dedication like no other sport.

Which gives me the background necessary as an authority to comment on any sports program which attempts to develop young men into responsible citizens. All college coaches have a tremendous responsibility to assure the leadership role in not only developing skilled football players by position but to realize the opportunity they have in guiding the development of responsible citizens of their players.

In today's society, winning the game is paramount in our value system. But the idea of winning is short-lived. Years later, one remembers how the game was won, not just the score. I have been observing the details of coaching procedure used by the Bluefield athletic program during this season.

Although I have never coached a team at a high school or university level, I have always assumed that a primary responsibility of a coach is to seek, find, and develop the skilled players at each position. Placing the best qualified player in each position gives any team the best chance of winning a given contest. I question if this has been the procedure followed during this season at the athletic program at Bluefield University. The third team passer for the current team has had outstanding success as an accurate long-distance passer—yet he has played only a few minutes in only three contests so far this season. His accuracy in passing long distances has made a significant contribution to Bluefield winning at least three contests—yet he is still on the player's chart as a third-string quarterback. The absence of Emmitt's passing ability could have contributed to Bluefield's loss to Comanche Gap.

My comments in this column are not intended to challenge the coach but only to ask for feedback on the coaching decisions made.

I am unable to comprehend the reasoning to use a skilled passer for only the last two or three minutes of a game when the outcome is in doubt. A player who receives such an assignment faces a "pressure-packed" period of performance although the Bluefield player receiving such assignments has performed exceedingly well in spite of this pressure. The player faces a defense which may cast aside the game plan and go all out to disrupt the passer's delivery. The pass receiver will likely face a determined effort by the secondary defense to intervene in the planned routing. And the offense would likely find their offensive scheme in disarray.

BLUEFIELD EAGLES
THE FOURTH GAME OF THE SEASON: FORT LUCAS
SEPTEMBER 24TH

The lineup for the next game had Jeff Gray returning as quarterback and Parker listed as questionable. As the players were introduced, Emmitt received a standing ovation that lasted for an extended period of time. The Fort Lucas team was known as a hard-running team with a ground game and limited passing. The first quarter ended with no score. With 8 minutes and 55 seconds remaining in the second quarter, Gray ran a bootleg play around the left end but was tackled by two Fort Lucas linemen. Gray did not immediately get up, and time-out was called. After a period of examination and discussion, Gray left the field, and Parker was sent in as his replacement. During the rest of the second quarter, neither team threw a pass nor scored a point.

Early during the third quarter, Parker had to leave the field due to an equipment problem, and Wilson was sent in as a replacement. With six minutes remaining in the third quarter, he completed an 83-yard pass—again to Fry. When the fourth quarter got under way, Parker resumed his position as quarterback. With seven minutes remaining in the quarter, Parker again had equipment problems and left the game. During the balance of the final quarter, Wilson completed a 66-yard pass, followed by a 39-yard touchdown pass. The

Eagles won the game 21 to 8. Wilson's success in this game seemed to predict his future.

You cannot have achievement without some form of accountability.

Rod Page

CHAPTER FIVE

WAYWARD WINDS OF A PROFESSION

CHAPTER FIVE

1. The Star Investigative Service Report

2. Reaction to the Report

3. Comments on Six-man Football

4. An Anonymous Email

5. UIL/ NCAA Six-man Football Rules Comparison

6. The National News Service

WAYWARD WINDS OF A PROFESSION

President Dr. Bowen had called a meeting of the Board of Regents to hear a report from the Star Investigative Services. The press had been invited to attend and hear the presentation by Rex Overton, president of Star Investigative Services.

Overton presented information regarding the background of the Star Investigative Services. He stated that the company had been in existence for over twelve years and had performed services throughout the southern part of the United States for universities, colleges, and high schools. Their staff was made up of retired FBI personnel as well as experienced investigative individuals from the University Interscholastic League and the Association of Sports Officials. His own background was service in the FBI for 23 years. He commented that the SIS had been placed on a timeline for a due date of its report and that their investigation had begun immediately.

Once the Star investigators received the background report on Emmitt Wilson, their team began their search for details of the activities leading up to the injury. They questioned the three doctors and received a statement from Head Coach Havens and then followed up with an individual conference with each assistant coach and selected team members.

The three doctors who were involved in the treatment of Emmitt Wilson were called upon first. Dr. Burrow, the team doctor, was asked to relate his involvement in the situation. He stated that he had not been present on the field when the accident occurred but had been sent for almost immediately. He stated that he found the player on the ground in a prone position. His helmet had been removed, and he was bleeding from his nose and both eyes. He immediately requested the player be sent to the University clinic on campus. Once the player reached the clinic and a limited further examination was performed, Dr. Burrow ordered that Emmitt be sent to the Regional Hospital. Once there, Dr. Burrow met with Dr. Jim Cowan—the neurology surgeon—and Dr. Gerald King—the orthopedic surgeon—who had been alerted to join him there in the emergency room.

Dr. Cowan did an extensive examination of Emmitt and expressed concern as to the extent of the damage done by blows received on each side of the head at almost the exact same time. Excessive bleeding had occurred and was continuing to some extent. He deemed the situation alarming and expressed deep concern as to the outcome.

Dr. Gerald King did a similar examination, and his conclusion was that the player had bruises in several parts of his body, but he observed no broken bones. However, the shoulder injury was a real concern.

The investigative team also asked for background information on Emmitt Wilson. They received information from college registration and the recruiting team which had been involved in all recruiting activities, past and present.

STAR INVESTIGATIVE SERVICES

To: Bluefield Board of Regents
From: The Star Investigative Services

Attached for you review and discussion please note the report concerning the Star Investigative Service's findings regarding the football scrimmage which took place on October 28th at the Bluefield University practice field.

STAR INVESTIGATIVE SERVICES

To: The University Board of Regents
Bluefield University

From: Star Investigative Services
Austin/San Antonio/New Orleans

Ref: Report Regarding a Football Practice Injury

During a routine football practice session of the Bluefield football team, Emmitt Wilson was severely injured and entered the hospital as a result. Dr. Donald Bowen, University President, requested the Star Investigative Service make an extensive investigation of the events during the practice as well as day-to-day activities leading up to this practice session.

BACKGROUND INFORMATION LEADING UP TO THE DATE OF PRACTICE

The Bluefield football squad had been divided into three teams designated as the first-team (the blue team), the second-team (the red team), and the third-team (the gray team). Team members not on any of these three designated teams served as substitutes for the three teams.

Emmitt Wilson is classified as a junior and has been a squad member since his freshman year. He is listed as the quarterback of the gray team. During his first two years on the squad, he was assigned to a defensive back position and had limited playing time.

The practice being investigated took place on Wednesday, October 28th, and was in preparation for a scheduled game with Comanche Gap. Scouting reports showed their team to be a talented passing team. Head Coach Havens was in the process of preparing a defense to meet their opponent's talented offense. Thus, Wednesday's practice was designed to protect against the Comanche Gap passing attack. The first (blue) and second (red) teams of Bluefield were to participate in the exercise. The red team was to represent Comanche Gap and be on the offense; the blue team was to represent Bluefield and be on the defense. However, Emmitt Wilson was designated to be quarterback of the offense representing Comanche Gap because of his passing skills.

With these assignments, the practice session was set. The Comanche Gap squad was to run pass play after pass play to test the effectiveness of the Bluefield pass defense. Some seven pass plays were run with the Bluefield defense not reaching the passer on any of these plays and with Wilson completing 88% of his passes. Coach Havens had directed the Bluefield defense and demonstrated his displeasure with the Bluefield defense. In the defensive huddle, he had directed all linemen and two of the three linebackers to rush the passer. According to the players in the huddle, the coach had commented that they were not earning their scholarships and that changes might be forthcoming.

During the running of the last play—the one in which Wilson was injured—players have said they heard Coach Havens say in a very loud voice, "Take him out of there! Hurt him!" This outburst is denied by Coach Havens; however, there is ample testimony to this as a fact.

The Star Investigative Service Committee had been given a deadline of five days to conduct the investigation and submit the findings. On the fifth day of this investigation, we received an anonymous email with the following message:

To: The Star Investigative Committee

Date: XXXXXXXXXXXXXX

The committee is hereby advised that Coach Havens maintains a second bank account in a different bank than his home account. During the last year, he had deposited $10,000 into this account. During this current year, he has deposited $20,000. These two deposits were made by cashier's checks.

This committee was concerned with the legitimacy of the email as well as its source. Due to the time restriction, the committee was unable to follow this lead—however, the committee felt they were obligated to present this information to the Board.

The SIS has been unable to determine why so much pressure was directed to the team for this particular game while no such pressure was apparent at other practice sessions this season. Also, why was the third- team quarterback directed to lead the second-team when the regularly assigned quarterback has far more experience at that position and was not injured at this time? Our only explanation is that the third-team quarterback (Wilson) has an outstanding record during his limited playing time this season, more so than anyone else on the team. Prior to this practice session, Coach Havens has been reluctant to recognize Wilson's ability.

There seems to be no doubt that Wilson was a "marked man" during this practice. He was not even wearing the usual red jacket to protect him as a quarterback. We were unfortunately unable to determine the reason behind such action. This may very well be a case of a coach targeting one of his own players.

Our conclusion is that there are other elements involved in this situation that we were unable to determine at this time due mainly to our time limit. A player was needlessly injured for a reason we have been unable to determine. We recommend further investigation into this matter be pursued. The Star Investigative Services is standing by to discuss any part of this report.

Rex Overton

Rex Overton

President

After hearing the Star Investigative Services report, the Board went into a general discussion without the public in attendance.

President Dr. Bowen—"Well, members, you have heard the SIS report. I would ask each of you to comment on your impression of the findings."

Mills—"Since I have heard the report, I have more questions than I had before the report was presented. I have always respected Coach Havens' team decisions, but I wonder about the reasoning behind these recent activities."

Daniels—"I am still shocked about what I termed was Coach Havens' lack of concern about Wilson's injuries when he did not get up after the pileup."

Ford—"That still bothers me too!"

Spurlock—"I cannot understand. Coach Havens seems to be playing down the extent and seriousness of Wilson's injuries."

McCorcle—"Coach has really been concerned about the game with Comanche Gap."

Mills—"That is true; however, it is not like him not to be concerned about a player's injuries. This report directed my attention to the assignment of Wilson to the red team. Dick Parker has had that position all season so far."

Chairman Peebles—"What is you reaction to the coach's outburst of 'Get him out of there! Hurt him!'?"

Spurlock—"It increased my concern about the targeting by the coach."

Mills—"I cannot believe a coach would do such a thing. But the thirty-thousand-dollar payment might prove to be the incentive."

Spurlock—"Havens does not have anything kind to say about six-man football. Why would he downplay that sport so much?"

Chairman Peebles—"What do you have reference to?"

Spurlock—"After Gray and Parker were knocked out of the Corpus game, Coach Havens told Coach Gilmore to go ahead and put 'what's his name' in to take over as quarterback. He then said, 'since we are on our own goal line, he can't hurt us much now.' That was just before Wilson threw the 100-yard pass."

Daniels—"That was the same night Havens told Massey that Wilson was not of the same quality as the other two quarterbacks."

Chairman Peebles interrupted the discussion. "Because six-man football has been referred to a number of times in these deliberations, we need to ask Herb Gormley to comment on some of the points of six-man football."

Gormley—"I have been involved in six-man football for a number of years. I played the game as a high school student for my freshman year through my senior year. I played for the Copperas Cove Bulldogs, which was a 'power-house'—winning their district championship during three of my four years there. In comparison to eleven-man football, I sight the following rules of procedure:

- *The game is played on a modified field which measures 80 yards by 40 yards.
- *Goal posts are 25 feet apart with the crossbar 9 feet above the ground.
- *The length of each quarter is 10 minutes with 2 minutes between quarters and 15 minutes between halves.
- *When one team is 45 or more points ahead at the end of the first half, the game is called and the winner declared.
- *The offense must advance the ball 15 yards instead of 10 yards in four downs in order to achieve a first down.

>*The offense must have at least 3 players on the line of scrimmage as the ball is snapped.

This list should give you a general idea of the game. It is a fast-moving game with almost continuous activity. A large amount of the blocking and tackling occurs in the open field. I will be happy to answer any questions which you may have at this time."

Mills—"Coach Havens seems to discount six-man experience altogether."

Gormley—"Dr. Bowen, may I make an additional statement reflecting some of the public's feelings about this entire situation?"

President Dr. Bowen—"Yes, Gormley, please do."

Gormley—"My contact with a number of the sports-minded public reflects that Wilson has been discriminated against because—of all things—his athletic ability and his six-man football experience."

Spurlock—"There is something that has not been brought to light in this situation, and whatever it is may be the key to the cause of this dilemma."

Ford—"I agree with that statement, but what could it be?"

Daniels—"Whatever it is, it is tied directly to Coach Havens."

Spurlock—"I cannot understand Havens' actions toward Wilson. I would think any coach who discovered a player with Wilson's talent would take him under his wing and make the most of his talents. The thing that got my attention was Havens not even knowing Wilson's name for so very long."

This meeting adjourned at this time in order for the Board to conduct a second meeting which had been scheduled involving the coaching staff and selected team members. The meeting was to be conducted in the Board of Regents Assembly Hall. The Board was to conduct this meeting which was to be a series of interviews in the executive chambers. The individual to be interviewed was to be called as scheduled to come before the Board on an individual basis. Jimmy Clark, a defensive lineman, was the first to be called to appear before the Board.

Chairman Peebles—"Jimmy, during a pass defense drill such as you were having that Wednesday, what is your assignment?"

Clark—"I was to charge across the line of scrimmage and disrupt the pass play."

Chairman Peebles—"How were you to disrupt the play?"

Clark—"Any way I could."

Chairman Peebles—"I understand that you were among the first players to reach the passer?"

Clark—"Yes, sir. I think that Tommy Mills and I arrived at about the same time."

Chairman Peebles—"What do you do in such a case when you reach the passer?"

Clark—"You tackle hard and drive the passer to the ground."

Chairman Peebles—"The blows that damaged Wilson were to the head. Could this be termed as targeting?"

Clark—"Maybe so—but we were not trying to hurt Wilson—only trying to please Coach Havens."

Chairman Peebles—"Do you normally practice this hard in scrimmages before a game?"

Clark—"No, sir! The scouting reports on Comanche Gap, our next opponent, had caused the coach's concern about the passing game."

Chairman Peebles—"Thank you, Jimmy. Would Ellis Fry please come to the conference table?"

Chairman Peebles—"Ellis, I believe you are listed on the position chart as a wide receiver?"

Fry—"Yes, sir. My primary duty is to run the pass routes and catch passes if they are thrown in my direction, or sometimes I may be assigned to blocking duties."

Chairman Peebles—"How are you classified?"

Fry—"I am classified as a junior."

Chairman Peebles—"I understand you have had some success in catching long passes?"

Fry—"Yes, sir. Wilson can throw the ball farther than anyone I have ever heard of—he is an excellent ball player. I hope he gets a scholarship next year."

Chairman Peebles—"You mean he is not on a scholarship?"

Fry—"No! He has played 3 years without any financial aid."

Chairman Peebles—"Some say Emmitt Wilson just throws the ball in almost any direction and you as a wide receiver run under it and make the catch."

Fry—"I suppose a part of that statement may be true, but the ball must be there before I can run under it. That is where Emmitt comes in. As far as I know, he is the only player I know who can deliver the ball at such far distances in order to make the long pass possible—let alone successful."

Fry continues—"Emmitt and the wide receivers have a code that I pass along each time we are in a position to predict the long pass. I indicate to Majors a message such as—the left goal post or the right goal post, or the left goal line corner, or the right goal line corner. Such designation is intended to guide their direction as they enter their passing patterns. It is not a definite designation but does guide me as I identify their direction as I look for their selected passing pattern. Each of us is involved in the execution. This is only the beginning initiation of a passing pattern, and circumstances dictate the execution of a pattern from this point forward."

Chairman Peebles—"Such directions seem vague and lack any definite direction."

Fry—"That may seem vague to outsiders, but it has been very successful with us during this season so far."

Chairman Peebles—"Ellis, let me ask you what you may consider an unfair question. Is Wilson liked by his team members?"

Fry—"During his freshman year, he was low key, but it was apparent that he wanted to be a student of the game. He wanted to understand the purpose and design of every play."

Fry continued—"As a sophomore, during the games he stood near the coach receiving the plays called from the press box. He made notes, and sometime at a later date he inquired as to why such a play was called. He had a thirst for knowledge about the game."

Chairman Peebles—"What did the coaching staff think about his 'outlaw' practice sessions?"

Fry—"In the beginning most of the staff made fun about the extra practice time. Making statements like—'We may not be working the regular practice tough enough for some of the players. If they have that much energy after our practice, maybe we need to practice tougher and for a longer period of time.' However, after a period of time when Majors and I joined the group at the 'outlaw' practice sessions, the coaches' attitude changed to an about face regarding the extra practice. Then when Majors and I began to haul in the long passes and win games, no longer was it a joke to them."

Fry—"Head Coach Havens never recognized it as a coaching activity—except to say that the outlaw practices were not to take place on the University practice field."

Fry—"With all of the joking and uncomplimentary comments about the 'outlaw' practice and Wilson, no one ever heard Wilson make any disrespectful comment concerning the coaching staff or any team player."

Chairman Peebles—"Thank you, Ellis. Would Jason Levy please come to the conference table?"

Chairman Peebles—"Jason, I believe you are the manager for the team?"

Levy—"Yes, sir."

Chairman Peebles—"Jason, please tell us what your job entails."

Levy—"I stay near the head coach and respond to his needs. For example, I take messages to the other coaches and have supplies available when needed."

Chairman Peebles—"When you say supplies, to what are you referring?"

Levy—"Tape, shoe strings, a play book, and any other item that is needed by the head coach or the assistant coaches."

Chairman Peebles—"When the head coach is huddling with one of the teams, are you nearby?"

Levy—"Yes, sir. I need to be near enough so that I can respond if he calls me."

Chairman Peebles—"The game coming up against Comanche Gap seems to be a pressure game. Is that true?"

Levy—"Yes, sir. It is! if we beat them, we have a real good chance of winning our conference. They have a very strong passing team."

Chairman Peebles—"This seems to have placed a lot of pressure on the coaches."

Levy—"Yes, sir—especially Coach Havens! He raises his voice and gets personal lately when he critiques players during practice."

Chairman Peebles—"Did Coach Havens yell during that practice and say 'Take him out! Hurt him!'?"

Levy—"Yes, sir. He did that the same day Wilson was hurt, but I don't think he meant it—he was just disappointed that the defense was not getting to the passer. Wilson was completing some of his passes even though the defense was trying to go all out to take him down."

Chairman Peebles—"Is Wilson liked by his team members?"

Levy—"Yes. He doesn't get to play much, but he is an excellent passer, and he does throw long passes. And he often compliments the offensive line for the protection they afford him when he is passing."

Chairman Peebles—"As good as Wilson is in the passing game, why do you think he doesn't get to play more?"

Levy—"I don't know. The team has wondered about that too. I suppose it's because Jeff Gray is the first-team quarterback."

Chairman Peebles—"Thank you, Jason. We may need to call on you again later. Would any member of the Regents care to have other members of the team provide any additional information? Tommy Watson, whom do you wish to speak to us?"

Watson—"I would like to have Leo Sims, the Athletic Director, appear before the Board."

Chairman Peebles—"Would Leo Sims please come forward and join us at the conference table? Mr. Watson, please proceed with any questions you might have."

Watson—"Coach Sims, how long have you served as Athletic Director at the University?"

Athletic Director Sims—"This is my seventh year."

Watson—"How long has Coach Havens been in the system here?"

Athletic Director Sims—"This is his fifth year."

Watson—"Has he been the head coach all of that time?"

Athletic Director Sims—"Yes, he has."

Watson—"How familiar are you with the pass defense drill that took place the day the quarterback was injured?"

Athletic Director Sims—"I was not present during the drill—but as soon as Wilson was hurt, they sent for me, and I came immediately."

Watson—"I have questions about the drill. Do you have this type of drill often? I mean, running the same play time and time again say for seven or eight straight times?"

Athletic Director Sims—"I don't know about that many. However, I do know that there was concern with the passing ability of Comanche Gap's quarterback."

Chairman Peebles—"Jim Carson, as coach of the defensive line, do you have a statement at this time?"

Carson—"Yes, I do. We seldom call defensive plays where we charge seven players, but this was an exception."

Athletic Director Sims—"Such a charge would be in more-or-less a desperate attempt to stop the progress of the opposing team."

Hernandez—"To me, it is most unusual for a team to have all five linemen as well as three linebackers all charge at the same time."

Athletic Director Sims—"Such a play could rob the secondary of its effectiveness in defending against long pass plays."

Chairman Peebles—"Thank you, Mr. Sims and Mr. Hernandez. Now would Coach Havens please come to the conference table?"

Chairman Peebles—"Coach Havens, the Board has a concern regarding your verbal reactions during the Wednesday practice session in question. I have reference to one play where your instruction to the defense was—and I quote—'Take him out of there! Hurt him!'"

Coach Havens—"I don't recall saying 'Hurt him!' I must have been misunderstood. I know I do get excited at times during practice, but I deny saying the 'Hurt him!' phrase."

Chairman Peebles—"Well, what about a play critique where after your comment of 'take him out,' one of your players said, 'He is one of us— we don't want to hurt him!' As I understand things, you responded by saying, 'He is not one of us! He is trying to defeat us! Get to him!'"

Coach Havens—"My thinking in that case was to have the practice be more meaningful by having our defensive players take this practice as a game situation and to concentrate on the purpose of the defensive charge."

Chairman Peebles—"Coach, what is your purpose when you participate in the defensive huddle?"

Coach Havens—"It makes me aware of the defense to be used when the next play is run. I am more able to observe the exact place the defense is concentrating on, and my critique of the play is more meaningful."

Chairman Peebles—"Your position chart indicates that you conduct your coaching activities with 3 designated teams. Is that correct?"

Coach Havens—"Yes. The teams are designated as the blue, red, and gray teams. The blue is the first team, the red is the next in line, while the gray is the third position."

Chairman Peebles—"The player who was injured—Emmitt Wilson—which team was he assigned to?"

Coach Havens—"He is a member of the gray team."

Chairman Peebles—"That would be the third team, correct?"

Coach Havens—"Yes."

Chairman Peebles—"Why would a third-team quarterback be directing the red team during the Wednesday scrimmage?"

Coach Havens—"He does have some passing ability, but he is not of the same caliber as the other two quarterbacks."

Chairman Peebles—"Coach, I have noticed while viewing the game films, that Wilson has completed a 100-yard pass winning the game, an 83-yard pass, and a 66-yard pass—again, winning the game—and a 43- yard pass together with a 36-yard pass—all within a 2 week period, and yet you say he is not of the same caliber as your other two quarterbacks?"

Coach Havens—"If you will examine further, you will see that he only had 6-man football experience in high school. This limits his knowledge of the game."

Chairman Peebles—"Thank you, Coach. We may want to talk with you again later on."

BLUEFIELD EAGLES
THE FIFTH GAME OF THE SEASON: ALABAMA TECH
OCTOBER 1ST

The lineup for the next game was the same original lineup for the season: Gray and Parker in the backfield with Fry as a wide receiver. After three quarters of play with the score Bluefield 14 and Alabama Tech 21, the crowd began to chant Wilson's name. The chant started off with a small section of the Bluefield student body but grew to even include the visitors' section chiming in. With seven minutes remaining in the game and the ball on the 11-yard line, Wilson was sent in to assume the quarterback position. The first play Bluefield called was a running play which resulted in a loss of 7 yards. The next play called was a pass play; however, Wilson was trapped behind the line with a loss of 3 yards. The next play was a pass play, and, with protection, Wilson was able to set his passing stance as Fry charged down the field and again fielded Wilson's throw as he crossed the goal line. Once again the crowd responded with great excitement. Wilson did not return to the lineup for the last two minutes of the game. The crowd was loud and showing its displeasure over this decision. Bluefield won the game with a final goal in the last two minutes of the game.

THE NATIONAL NEWS SERVICE
SPORTS REVIEW

by

HERB GORMLEY

It is Monday at the Bluefield University after the scrimmage of all scrimmages. The quarterback (third string) has regained consciousness and is no longer drifting into unconsciousness on a daily basis. This is considered a hopeful sign toward his recovery.

Much has been learned regarding the background and developments of this unfortunate day of a football scrimmage. First of all, it seems that quarterback Emmitt Wilson had been working hard to overcome the "stigma" of having played six-man football while attending Sparta High School. Although Sparta High had won its district and regional titles for three years in a row while Wilson played the position of quarterback and had an outstanding record while guiding the team, Wilson was still not considered a competent quarterback by Coach Havens.

Wilson came to Bluefield University and enrolled without a scholarship. Here three years later, he still has no scholarship. He played a defensive position his first two years, and only in his third year was he moved to the third team quarterback position. He is paying his way through the university by serving as a student janitor at the chemistry building, a job which pays for his room and board.

The coaching staff implies that he is a successful passer, but he does not always follow the playbook passing patterns—and that Coach Havens is a stickler who insists that only plays in the playbook can be used at all times. For example, the 100-yard pass play Wilson made was not in the playbook—nor was his 83-yard pass.

Also, the coaching staff does not necessarily condemn his "self-practices" or "outlaw" practice sessions as the coaching staff refers to them. Emmitt takes part in these sessions after regularly scheduled practice time as well as on weekends and holidays. The main theme of these "outlaw" practices is to work on improving timing of different aspects of an individual play as well as variations of different passing patterns. He seems to have no problem enlisting passing partners to take part in these activities. Evidently, the head coach did not even know his name until the current scrimmage—and has even referred to him a number of times as "what's his name."

It is difficult to believe that a prospective player with the talents Emmitt Wilson possesses would receive this kind of treatment and non-recognition from his own team. This columnist wishes Emmitt a complete recovery and the recognition he deserves.

When I was in school during the fifties and sixties, the only terrorist we knew was the high school principal.

Hugy Harris

CHAPTER SIX

WAYWARD WINDS OF A PROFESSION

CHAPTER SIX

1. Wilson's Condition

2. Discussion of the First Anonymous Email

3. A Second Anonymous Email

4. False Observer Assumptions

5. The Source of the Deposits

6. The Second 100-yard Pass

WAYWARD WINDS
OF A PROFESSION

Three days later, chairman Peebles contacted the Board members to inform them that Emmitt Wilson had gone 48 hours without lapsing into unconsciousness. Dr. Burrow was hopeful that this was a definite indication of improvement in his condition. However, there was still a deep concern as to the possibility that the lapses might return.

Peebles scheduled a board meeting for the following day to visit with Coach Havens concerning the anonymous email he had received about the bank deposits. At the scheduled date and time, the meeting of the Board of Regents was called to order.

Chairman Peebles—"Coach Havens, during the time the Star Investigative Services committee was involved in its investigation, they received an email regarding two of your bank deposits."

A copy of the following email was given to Coach Havens as well as to each board member:

To: The Star Investigative Committee

Date: XXXXXXXXX

> The committee is hereby advised that Coach Havens maintains a second bank account in a different bank than his home account. During this last year, he has deposited $10,000 into this account. During this current year, he has also deposited $20,000. These two deposits were made by cashier's check.

Coach Havens—"Well, first of all, I think this is a personal matter and the Board has no business in becoming involved in my personal business."

Chairman Peebles—"The Board realizes this is personal business, and we apologize for the invasion of your personal affairs. However, in view of our involvement in the football scrimmage incident, our feeling is that if there is a simple explanation, we can put all the rumors to rest before they become a major issue in the community."

Coach Havens—"Well, I will say again, it is none of the Regents' business, and I resent your invasion into my personal life. But in order to put the rumors to rest, I will inform you that my mother owned rural property, and after her death several years ago, I decided to sell the property—thus, my deposits after the sale of the property."

Chairman Peebles—"We appreciate you providing us this information, and again, I apologize for the intrusion into your personal business. Please forgive us."

Coach Havens then left the meeting somewhat upset and openly commented that this invasion of his personal business and the rumors it had started had disrupted the concentration of both the coaching staff and the team.

McCorcle—"His explanation seems reasonable, but I wish he had offered to supply some evidence of the sale of the property at some future date."

Cloud—"That would have given proof of the transaction thereby removing any doubt."

Spurlock—"I am willing to accept his explanation and let the matter go."

The following afternoon, a second anonymous email was received in the University President's office which was addressed to the Board of Regents. The email contained additional information concerning Coach Havens' second bank account.

President Dr. Bowen called the University attorney and asked for a recommended procedure. The attorney advised that the matter should be brought before the Board.

As this meeting was preparing to adjourn, Dr. Bowen's secretary entered the room with an apology for interrupting the meeting and presented a paper to Dr. Bowen.

President Dr. Bowen spoke after reading the paper. "Board members, there is more disturbing news with another anonymous email. Allow me to read it to you:

To: The Board of Regents, Bluefield University

Date: XXXXXXXX

> The two deposits made to Coach Havens' bank account were from the parent of one of the current members of the football team.

Each member of the Board received a copy of the email which caused uncontrolled expressions of disbelief. The meeting was adjourned with another Board meeting scheduled for the next day.

At the next meeting of the Board of Regents, the emails were discussed.

Spurlock—"If this is true, the coach just stood before us and made false statements or outright lied to the Board of Regents."

Hernandez—"Why would he do such a thing? What or who is he trying to protect?"

Chairman Peebles—"This is a disturbing development which is going to have a major impact on the Board's investigation!"

Spurlock—"Just when I had committed to letting the charges go!"

Chairman Peebles—"This development calls for another meeting with Coach Havens—this time, not so cordial!"

McCorcle—"The anonymous emails amount to a strange development in my opinion. Somebody is really after Havens!"

Spurlock—"What concerns me is the fact that the sender of these emails seems to have a pipeline into our meetings."

Cloud—"My first guess as to who the sender might be was a member of the coaching staff, but that doesn't seem feasible now."

Chairman Peebles—"I am concerned that we are placing so much emphasis on these anonymous emails. Yet, the implication—if true—can have a profound impact on the University."

Spurlock—"Yes, I agree that we have no choice other than to conduct a more intense investigation."

Cloud—"This will have far-reaching and disturbing effects on our personnel."

Chairman Peebles—"We need to contact the university attorney and have him guide us through our next procedure. Once I have had dialogue with him, I will schedule our next meeting."

At a meeting with attorney Mark Woods, Chairman Peebles updated him on the Board receiving a second anonymous email. Woods suggested he should meet with the entire Board of Regents for a detailed discussion.

As attorney Woods began his meeting with the Board members, he cautioned them about false obvious assumptions. "The fact that the situation started with an anonymous email is legally a weak position to be placed in; however, we must keep in mind that the second email does not prove anything yet. The strongest point of the case against Coach Havens so far is the fact that he lied to the Board in identifying the source of the deposits. As of yet, we still do not know the identity of the individual who supposedly furnished the cash for the deposits into Havens' account. I now need direction from the Board as to the next step you wish to take. Is the Board interested in building a case against Havens, or are you just concerned with attempting to identify the source of the bank account information?"

Chairman Peebles—"What are our choices?"

Attorney Woods—"The bank account statement which I think started the situation we now find ourselves in is really none of our business—I am speaking only of the bank account statement—the statement did provide a concern to you—however, the bank is the one to follow through as to who violated the bank's principles of privacy—not you."

Attorney Woods continued—"Another primary concern is the welfare of Emmitt Wilson. There are implications that Wilson was purposely sacrificed for some unknown reason. That could be a huge, huge problem for the University."

Spurlock—"Why the University? We had no hand in the scrimmage."

Attorney Woods—"You had every hand in the situation. Coach Havens was your representative in the scrimmage."

McCorcle—"I don't understand your reasoning there. We were not at the scrimmage. We were not consulted in any way. After all, we are on the Board as a public service."

Attorney Woods—"You are the ones anyone who brings a suit will charge—believe me!"

Cloud—"Well then, can we sue Havens?"

Attorney Woods—"In my opinion, your only recourse there is to dismiss him."

Chairman Peebles—"I believe our next step should be to meet with Coach Havens and at least give him a chance to explain his actions at our last meeting. Mr. Woods, we request that you be present and conduct any questioning which you deem advisable. If we are all in agreement, I will make the necessary arrangements."

After consulting with attorney Mark Woods, chairman Peebles scheduled the next Board of Regents meeting for 9:00 a.m. the following day.

After calling the meeting to order, the questioning began.

Chairman Peebles—"Coach Havens, we have scheduled this meeting in order to obtain additional information from you regarding deposits made in one of your bank accounts."

Coach Havens—"I am at a loss as to why my bank statement is such a concern for the Board. As I stated in the previous meeting, I do not think it is any of the Board's business. I am tempted to just walk out of this meeting and go about my assigned duties of coaching football."

Chairman Peebles—"Coach, you may certainly do that. It is your decision. However, it could mean that you are also walking out of your employment with this University."

Coach Havens—"Please tell me why such a small bit of information is such a big deal with this Board!"

Chairman Peebles—"That is exactly what this meeting will explore! We have asked the University attorney, Mark Woods, to conduct the next phase of this meeting."

Attorney Woods—"Coach Havens, the Board is asking you to look upon this meeting as a fact-finding mission which will require your cooperation in presenting the facts in reference to the questions to be discussed."

Coach Havens—"You mean this meeting could have a bearing on my employment with the University?"

Attorney Woods—"It is possible."

Coach Havens—"I had no idea the situation was that serious!"

Attorney Woods—"Recent developments have caused some of your previous testimony to now be in question. We have reason to believe your statements made at the last meeting were not honest and straightforward."

Coach Havens—"Are you implying that I lied in answering questions posed at the last meeting?"

Attorney Woods—"That is what we plan to determine in this meeting."

Coach Havens—"I'll have you know that I have no reason to lie and I refuse to give further details concerning my bank accounts!"

Attorney Woods—"We were in hopes that you could substantiate your statement about the sale of your mother's property with a bill of sale or some other legal document regarding the sale."

Coach Havens—"No! It is none of the Board's business, and I refuse to give further details concerning the sale! How could such a sale have anything to do with Wilson's injury?"

Attorney Woods—"One reason for our concern is based on the fact of a second anonymous email the Board received yesterday afternoon."

At that point, the attorney presented Coach Havens with a copy of the email. It revealed that the two deposits to Havens' account were from the parent of a current team member.

Coach Havens—"You mean you are basing all this inquiry into my personal business on the anonymous emails? I refuse to continue this dialogue!"

Chairman Peebles—"Coach, you might want to make a choice—either cooperate here with the Board or have the next meeting with the District Attorney."

Coach Havens—"Chairman Peebles, I consider your statement to be a threat, and as long as your charges against me are based on anonymous emails, they will not stand up in a court of law. I believe I now have grounds to sue the University!"

At this point, Havens stormed out of the meeting. The board members and Woods remained in the meeting room for further discussion.

Spurlock—"Board members, we seem to have a tiger by the tail!"

Attorney Woods—"He is correct in saying that without evidence of the identity of the source of the emails, our case is lacking meaningful evidence."

Chairman Peebles—"At least it is putting pressure on Havens to provide additional information."

The following day at approximately 9:40 a.m., President Dr. Bowen received a phone call from a person who only identified himself as a parent of a current football team member. The individual asked to meet privately with Dr. Bowen and the Board of Regents chairman, Lee Peebles. Peebles stated that under the current circumstances, he felt that the entire Board of Regents should be present. The caller readily agreed to this arrangement, and a time was set for 2:00 p.m. that same afternoon in the executive conference room. The parent turned out to be Marvin Gray, the father of the first team quarterback, Jeff Gray.

President Dr. Bowen welcomed Mr. Gray and asked that he explain his reason for requesting such a meeting.

Mr. Gray—"Gentlemen, I appreciate your willingness to meet with me so quickly. I think you will find my mission to be of paramount interest to the University and especially to the athletic department."

Chairman Peebles—"Please continue."

Mr. Gray—"I feel you should know that I have informed Coach Havens of my asking for this meeting. I must say that he is violently opposed to this meeting. However, in the interest of the welfare of the athletic department and perhaps even the whole University, I feel this meeting must take place."

After a short pause, Mr. Gray continued—"I am the person who made the two payments to Coach Havens. I had consulted with an attorney who advised me that there was nothing illegal about my making such payments. However, now I have a concern about the ethics of this action. My son's grandfather had played professional football a number of years ago, and the two of us had hoped that Jeff might follow in his footsteps."

Gray continued—"When I first offered the monetary gift to Coach Havens, he was hesitant to accept the funds. I explained to him that I was impressed with the performance of his coaching duties. I stated that I thought he was underpaid and since I was fortunate to be in a position financially where I could help the situation, I would like to make a contribution. He reluctantly accepted."

Mr. Gray—"I now realize that my actions involving financial payments place me, my family, and certainly Jeff in a bad light. This is especially true since Emmitt Wilson was injured during the recent scrimmage. I cannot understand but can only imagine the details which preceded the events leading up to and including this scrimmage."

After another pause, Mr. Gray continued—"At this time, I will answer any questions which the president and members of the Board of Regents may have."

Spurlock—"If you were under the impression that there was no legal problem with the payment of the funds to the coach, why all the secrecy?"

Mr. Gray—"Coach Havens thought it would be best that way."

Spurlock—"Did he say why he thought it would be best?"

Mr. Gray—"He was concerned with the morale of the coaching staff."

Williams—"This information makes me wonder about some of the position assignments during the scrimmage."

Spurlock—"I can certainly understand that!"

McCorcle—"I feel that Emmitt has been used to promote someone else."

Ford—"I feel that Emmitt knew or suspected some of this 'hush-hush' but never said a word about how he was treated."

Chairman Peebles—"Mr. Gray, did Coach Havens request that the funds you gave him be made by cashier's checks?"

Mr. Gray—"Yes, he did."

Chairman Peebles—"Mr. Gray, am I correct in assuming that you had no contact with Coach Havens after the date of the payments?"

Mr. Gray—"Yes. Other than the time he informed me by phone of the recruiter from a professional team requesting to view the game films."

Chairman Peebles—"Are there any more questions from the members of the Board of Regents? There being none, I wish to thank Mr. Gray for coming forward with this information. His comments will be most helpful to us as we continue our investigation. I ask the Board to remain for additional discussion of this new turn of events after a fifteen minute recess."

Mr. Gray leaves, and the Board returns after the break.

Chairman Peebles—"As members of the Board, you may be as surprised as I was at the information we just received."

Mills—"I am amazed at this turn of events! For Havens to be involved in such a thing is hard for me to believe!"

Hernandez—"It has brought to light why Wilson has not played more than he has!"

Chairman Peebles—"This information leads me to believe that Havens' accepting the 'gift' had a direct relation to the limited time which Wilson was allowed to play. I feel the coach definitely was fearful of Wilson overshadowing Gray in his performance as quarterback and thus affecting Jeff's possible selection by a professional team."

Williams—"Havens was trying to earn his thirty pieces of silver!"

THE BOARD'S DILEMMA

The receipt of the two anonymous emails, one to the Star Investigative Service and another to the Regional Board—both concerning activities of the Bluefield University head coach—placed the Board in quite a dilemma.

An anonymous instrument has little or no value in enforcing any legal action. Without the source of such accusation, the instrument could only serve as a "wake-up call" as to the need for further investigation into a given matter. Even when the Board thought to give the coach an opportunity to place the "rumors" at rest, his angry reply was "you mean you are basing your inquiry on anonymous information?" His meaning was interpreted as implying he would not dignify the question with an answer.

Although the Board had a legitimate concern as to the source of the charges made, their first decision was to not pursue the matter.

BLUEFIELD UNIVERSITY
THE SIXTH GAME OF THE SEASON: TULSA UNIVERSITY
OCTOBER 17, XXXX

THE SECOND 100-YARD PASS

The sixth game of the season was with Tulsa University and was an away game for the Bluefield Eagles; however, the stands were filled with Bluefield fans. As the game progressed, Tulsa players were giving a better than expected account of themselves. The game was tied at the half, and during the third quarter, Tulsa pulled ahead of Bluefield by a touchdown and an extra point. Well into the fourth quarter, Tulsa scored a field goal and led Bluefield by ten points. With 3 minutes and 4 seconds left in the game, Emmitt was sent in to play. On the second play, Emmitt was able to set his passing stance and completed a pass to Fry on the Tulsa 3-yard line. This meant with one minute and three seconds remaining in the game, Bluefield trailed by three points. Tulsa was held to no points for three plays and fumbled on Bluefield's three-yard line. One unsuccessful play later, Emmitt again called for the long pass. This time with the clock quickly running out, Emmitt tried a new pattern of escape. When the hard-charging Tulsa line rapidly closed off his avenue to take a passing stance, he charged toward the rushing linemen which surprised them, and he was able to take a stance within three yards of the line of scrimmage. This time his pass was received by Majors as he crossed the two-yard line. ANOTHER 100-YARD PASS, AND BLUEFIELD WON THE GAME BY A SCORE OF 21 TO 17.

POSITION PERFORMANCE EVALUATION

During the sixth game with Tulsa University, Jim Carson—the offensive line coach—had been alarmed at the blocking of two of Bluefield's offensive line positions. Two defensive players had displayed limited success in the area of the Bluefield offensive line as to their blocking assignments on pass defense. On a number of plays, they had been outmaneuvered by the defensive position which they were assigned to block. The defensive player across from the Bluefield right guard as well as the defensive player charging the Bluefield right guard had reached Emmitt only seconds after he had released his pass. Only a split second after Emmitt released his pass had Emmitt been tackled and piled on after he hit the ground. The situation was addressed during the practice on Tuesday. The Bluefield guard was replaced while the Bluefield tackle assigned to block the defensive showed improvement. However, the situation was still a concern of the Bluefield coaching staff.

On Monday following the sixth game of the season, Coach Havens received a communication from the New Orleans Saints Professional Headquarters asking permission to come by and view some of the game and practice films involving the passing plays of the Eagles. Coach Havens was pleased with the request and arranged for a viewing on the Monday of the following week.

Two individuals from the Saints organization arrived and were greeted by Coach Havens. They introduced themselves as John Carol and Raymond Hood. Havens advised them that he had parts of four different games and two practice sessions set up for their viewing. After viewing a part of the first two films, Raymond Hood stated, "These films show your quarterback, Jeff Gray. We would especially like to see films involving Emmitt Wilson."

Coach Havens—"Oh! I am surprised! Jeff Gray has been our starting quarterback for the last two years, and we won the conference both years. Emmitt Wilson is only our third-string quarterback."

Hood—"I believe from what we have heard that it is Wilson who throws the long passes?"

Coach Havens—"That is true. Very well. I will rearrange the films. It will take me just a few minutes."

Hood—"After viewing these films, I think we would like a copy of the two practice films. Would that be possible?"

Coach Havens—"Yes. I can send you copies within the week."

While preparing the film shipment to the New Orleans professional team, Havens commented to Athletic Director Leo Sims, "Wilson is not the exceptional passer he is made out to be! All he can do is throw a long ball—his success comes when Fry or Majors runs under it and scores. It is their speed that makes his success possible."

Athletic Director Sims—"That may be true to some extent, but the ball must be there before Fry or Majors can run under it."

Athletic Director Sims again—"Coach, what is your hang up with Wilson? He is a pro-caliber passer even now—however, you do not take advantage of his talent until defeat stares the team in the face."

Coach Havens—"Why do you say that?"

Athletic Director Sims—"Why do I say that? There are a lot of people saying that including some of the team members, your staff, and a multitude of the fans."

Coach Havens—"I cannot see that!"

Athletic Director Sims—"When you refer to him as 'a flash in the pan,' 'what's his name,' or 'lucky you are damaging your own reputation. People are asking why you do such a thing."

Coach Havens—"Let's get one thing settled right now! You take care of your athletic duties, and I will handle the football coaching!"

Athletic Director Sims—"That can happen as long as you are aware that you perform your duties in line with my policies and follow them. You work under my supervision, and as of now you are making some decisions that are outside of your job description and are damaging the entire athletic department. I have tried to support you in the operation of the Bluefield football program, but you are making it exceedingly hard to do it during this season."

Coach Havens—"I don't mean to step out of line, but I am trying to do what is best for the program."

Athletic Director Sims—"It is common talk around the University that you must have an ulterior motive behind your recent actions."

Coach Havens—"What could it be?"

Athletic Director Sims—"I suggest you think long and hard about this matter."

There is a difference in the people who make a difference.

> Norman Hall

CHAPTER SEVEN

WAYWARD WINDS OF A PROFESSION

CHAPTER SEVEN

1. Another Meeting with the Board of Regents and Havens

2. The Third 100-yard Pass

3. Student Involvement

4. A Proposal from a Professional Team

WAYWARD WINDS OF A PROFESSION

The Board of Regents assembled at 10:00 a.m. for discussion purposes. Coach Havens was scheduled to appear at 11:00.

Chairman Peebles—"Well, Board members, since the individual who made financial 'gifts' to coach Havens has identified himself, I feel Coach Havens has much to explain concerning his use of Emmitt Wilson as a quarterback during the current football season. What are your feelings and comments?"

Mills—"This development certainly places the coach in a bad light."

Ford—"In a really bad light! This can explain some questionable decisions and assignments he made."

McCorcle—"I am beginning to think the worst about some of Havens' coaching decisions."

Williams—"What about the person who supplied the copy of Havens' bank account? Is there any way we can bring pressure to identify this person?"

Chairman Peebles—"I appreciate your concern. However, the identity of the source of the 'gifts' to Havens is vital to our next step. According to attorney Woods, the identity of the person who supplied us the copy is a matter for the bank to pursue, not us."

Coach Havens arrived at the conference room promptly at 11:00 a.m.

Chairman Peebles—"Thank you, coach, for your on-time appearance. As you are aware, we have had recent developments in our investigation which will necessitate additional questions directed to you."

Spurlock—"Coach, I am surprised and disappointed that you would appear before this group and misrepresent the truth like I think you did at our last meeting."

McCorcle—"Coach, this I did not expect from you!"

Chairman Peebles—"Coach, from all the evidence which has been revealed to us, you placed Emmitt Wilson in harm's way with the intention of insuring his injury."

Coach Havens—"Quarterback Gray had brought us to two winning seasons and on the verge of a third. I thought we owed him the starting position."

Ford—"Maybe so! But to purposely injure another player to insure Gray the starting position? That is not right!"

Coach Havens—"I did not purposely get him hurt! That is a chance that all players take when they go out for the football team."

Hernandez—"Did I hear you say you did not purposely get Wilson hurt? Yet you were heard saying to the defense in a loud voice, 'Take him out of there! Hurt him!' What did you expect to happen?"

Coach Havens—"Yes! You know I did not do it on purpose!"

Hernandez—"No, I do not know that! As I understand the scrimmage procedure, during practice the quarterback wears a red jersey to ensure that he is identified to the defense that—as team members say—he is not scrimmage bait—which means he should not be tackled or hit during the scrimmage. Is this true?"

Coach Havens—"That is normally the procedure."

Hernandez—"Why was that not done during the Wednesday scrimmage?"

Coach Havens—"Because of our next opponent's passing ability, we wanted the scrimmage to be more realistic."

Hernandez—"So you purposely left off the red jersey? That set Wilson up for intentional injury!"

McCorcle—"If you were trying to be more realistic in this scrimmage, I would think you would have played our best players."

Coach Havens—"Yes! Certainly!"

McCorcle—"Then why was Dick Parker not playing? Isn't he the second-team quarterback rather than Emmitt Wilson?"

Coach Havens—"Wilson is a better passer than Parker."

McCorcle—"If Parker had been playing quarterback on the offense during this scrimmage, would you have yelled 'Take him out of there! Hurt him!'"

Coach Havens—"I did not say 'Hurt him!' I was misunderstood. I said 'hit him.'"

Spurlock—"I believe we can get at least a dozen people who were at the scrimmage to say they heard the words 'hurt him' when you were yelling to the defense line."

Coach Havens—"I know what I said!"

Chairman Peebles—"As a result of Mr. Gray's statements, I would be inclined to believe you had a selfish motive or reason to favor Jeff Gray over Emmitt Wilson."

Coach Havens—"Are you implying that the Board is in a position to make better decisions than the coaching staff?"

Attorney Woods—"Coach, getting back to the $30,000 payments you received from Mr. Marvin Gray, did you consider this a gift or payment for services rendered or just how did you classify the money you received?"

Coach Havens—"I considered it a 'thank you' statement for the time and training I had given to Jeff."

Williams—"Did you receive such a payment from any of the other players or their parents?"

Coach Havens—"No!"

Williams—"Did you expect such payments from the other parents or players?"

Coach Havens—"Certainly not!"

Williams—"Do I understand that because you received a payment from Mr. Gray that you gave Jeff more training than other players?"

Coach Havens—"This meeting now is exactly the reason I did not want the money from Mr. Gray—I knew it would be misinterpreted just as you are doing now! I did not dislike the 'boy,' but Jeff Gray has been the team quarterback for going on three years, and no 'flash in the pan' was going to damage his reputation!"

Williams—"I don't think I am misinterpreting anything!"

Chairman Peebles—"Coach Havens, do you admit that you received two payments of $10,000 and then $20,000 from Mr. Marvin Gray?"

Coach Havens—"Yes, sir."

Chairman Peebles—"Coach Havens, would you like to make any kind of statement before the meeting is adjourned?"

Coach Havens—"No, not at this time."

Chairman Peebles—"Coach Havens, it is becoming harder to not believe some of your coaching decisions were based on the so-called thirty pieces of silver that you received."

Chairman Peebles—"I will close this phase of our meeting at this time and excuse Coach Havens. I ask the Board of Regents to remain for an extended meeting."

The meeting of the Board of Regents continues after Coach Havens' departure.

Chairman Peebles—"Well, attorney Woods, where does this meeting leave the Board of Regents?"

Attorney Woods—"I think you are in a strong position to take almost any action relating to the coaching staff."

Chairman Peebles—"What do you think the coach's next step will be?"

Spurlock—"Do you feel that he thinks his job is on the line?"

Attorney Woods—"Yes! I think that he is concerned with job security, or at least he should be."

Williams—"What does his contract say? How many years does it read?"

Attorney Woods—"This is his first year of a three-year contract."

Mills—"Are we stuck with this situation for two more years of his coaching?"

Attorney Woods—"Not if we can show cause for breaking the contract."

Hernandez—"I think Emmitt Wilson was 'set up' by Havens to be injured."

Williams—"It seems to me that the fact that no red jersey was called for during this scrimmage points directly to that fact."

Spurlock—"The 'thirty pieces of silver' seem to be the source of this entire situation."

Cloud—"By your reference to 'thirty pieces of silver' I assume you mean the thirty thousand dollar 'gift' from Marvin Gray to Havens?"

Spurlock—"Yes!"

McCorcle—"I have always thought he was an above average coach, but his treatment of Wilson and his reason for many of his decisions is inexcusable and cannot be forgiven."

Attorney Woods—"Keep in mind that his decisions as to the use of personnel and their position assignments are within his job description and are legal. It is his acceptance of the financial payments that weakens his case. We must be able to show that the payments were the reason for Wilson's assignments and especially his assignment at the Wednesday scrimmage."

Mills—"The publicity the coach will get from this incident will not be good for his future."

Attorney Woods—"I feel sure that his attorney will not inform him—but win or lose, this case will damage his coaching career. I suggest we delay any further action by this Board until we are able to determine Havens' next step."

Chairman Peebles—"I agree. Do we have any Board members who disagree? None? Then let's adjourn this meeting at this time and see what tomorrow brings."

The meeting was adjourned. However, it broke into several conversations with two or three people—all concerning Emmitt Wilson's progress and predictions as to his future progress. It was also noted that the football team continued to practice for the season's final two scheduled games.

BLUEFIELD EAGLES
THE SEVENTH GAME OF THE SEASON: UNIVERSITY OF THE PERMIAN BASIN
OCTOBER 22ND

The lineup for the next game followed the usual pattern of position assignments: Gray and Parker in the backfield with Fry and Mobley as wide receivers. The Basin team had surprised the other conference team members by presenting an effective passing attack so far in the games played. More than half of their scoring had come as the result of their passing attack. However, their pass defense was not of the same caliber. Their ground game was their strongest asset. At half time, the Basin led by a score of 21-6. Gray had completed a number of 15- and 20-yard passes, but the team had been unable to follow with an effective running game. During the second half, Bluefield was able to score on a short fifteen-yard pass, and the ground game had produced another touchdown. But the score stood at Basin 28 and Bluefield 20. With 3 minutes and 11 seconds remaining in the game, Wilson was sent in to replace Gray. The crowd went wild with a roar of approval.

On the first play after Wilson assumed the quarterback position, a running play produced 7 yards. The next play—a running play—produced 6 yards. The Basin had a surprisingly effective pass rush which presented a problem for Bluefield. On the next play, the Basin rush forced Wilson to retreat to his own five-yard line before he was downed. On the next play, the offensive line was able to hold for an additional 5 seconds giving Wilson enough time to set his stance and **complete a pass to Fry as he crossed the three-yard line and scored.**

This made the score Basin 28 and Bluefield 27 with two minutes and 20 seconds left in the game. Bluefield tried an onside kickoff which failed, and Basin recovered the ball on the Bluefield 43-yard line. Basin threw two incomplete passes then tried a field goal which was wide of the goal.

Bluefield threw two short passes placing the line of scrimmage at Basin's 38-yard line. Bluefield was successful in their field goal attempt and won the game 30 to 28.

On Saturday afternoon after the seventh game with Permian Basin, the Board of Regents assembled for a general discussion meeting. There was no formal agenda. It was a meeting to discuss any items of interest.

THE THIRD 100-YARD PASS

It was noted that Wilson had just completed **ANOTHER** 100-yard pass with little or no recognition from Coach Havens.

It was noted that the Athletic Director should exercise more control over the head coach. There was a comment asking why he had not done so before now. One answer was that since he had been a winning coach for two years plus being successful this year, it might prove to be more difficult to take the situation in hand. To which one response had been winning at any cost was not the role of the University.

A group of three team members had gone to one of the University counselors asking for guidance in how to make a complaint concerning the way Emmitt Wilson was being treated. The group pointed out to the counselor that Emmitt must be aware of his unprofessional treatment—but he had never uttered a word of criticism toward the coaching staff and especially not toward Coach Havens. Even quarterback Gray was feeling uncomfortable about the turn of events.

Little else was discussed during the meeting other than a plan to bring the situation to a close as soon as possible.

As members of the Board of Regents went their separate ways, Dr. Bowen invited attorney Mark Woods and Chairman Lee Peebles to visit over coffee for an informal get-together. Dr. Bowen started the discussion by commenting that the situation was fast getting out of hand and that he was of the opinion that the Athletic Director had been derelict in the performance of his duties.

Attorney Mark Woods responded by stating: "It could seem so; however, Havens has had an outstanding record the past two years and until this turn of events surfaced, I could understand where the Athletic Director might be hesitant to make corrective statements concerning such a successful program."

Chairman Peebles—"I can understand your reasoning, but I feel that there was ample time for the A.D. to get involved even with the fast development of events."

Attorney Woods—"The knowledge of the event is going to snowball since the Heart Newspaper chain has sent two reporters into the community as a fact-finding team to develop stories. I dare say they will not be as understanding to the situation as Gormley has been."

Chairman Peebles—"I need your cooperation in bringing this situation to a close as soon as possible. I will appreciate any help you can provide."

The last comment of the meeting was: "And with all of this going on, Coach Havens thinks he is mistreated!"

With that comment, the meeting adjourned.

A PROPOSAL FROM A PROFESSIONAL TEAM

Three days after Emmitt had thrown his third 100-yard pass, Leo Sims, the athletic director at Bluefield University, received a call from the office of the New Orleans Saints organization asking for a chance to visit the Bluefield Athletic Department. Sims made an appointment for the following afternoon. At the appointed time, Carl Tipton appeared and introduced himself as a vice president of personnel for the New Orleans Saints Professional Football Organization. His purpose was to discuss a future draft choice from the Bluefield football squad.

Tipton's proposal was that the Saints would draft Emmitt Wilson during his junior year and leave him in the University for his junior and senior years thereby drafting him at the end of his senior year. This is a legal procedure and is done from time to time. Tipton's questions were about the character of Wilson and if Sims thought he would honor such a proposal. If not, the Saints did not want to waste a draft choice.

Sims' reaction to the proposal was that of surprise, but he asked for a delay in making the proposal to Wilson. He stated that he would like to talk to Wilson and his parents before asking Wilson to make a decision.

Tipton accepted the delay in having the decision made and asked to be informed once a decision was finalized.

Most people—teachers and administrators included—do not understand how learning happens.

Gale Bartow

CHAPTER EIGHT

WAYWARD WINDS OF A PROFESSION

CHAPTER EIGHT

1. Game Preparation for Comanche Gap

2. The Scrimmage

3. The Second Injury

4. Eighth Game of the Season

5. The National News Service

WAYWARD WINDS OF A PROFESSION

PREPARATION FOR THE COMANCHE GAP GAME

Preparations for the Comanche Gap game had all the "ear marks" of a playoff contest. Although it was three games away from such a decisive event, according to the local and state sports news, the winner of this game would most likely go on to win the conference championship. Thus, a more than usual serious nature was present in all phases of coaching assignments.

THE SCRIMMAGE

The preparations for game eight had the team returning somewhat to normal. The first-and second-team members now occupied their assigned positions, and the normal practice routine was under way. The next game's opponent—Comanche Gap—was a team which scouting reports revealed used passing plays some 43% of the time and ground plays the balance of the time. Coach Havens called the first-and second-team squads together and repeated the findings of the scouting report. He stated that the opposing quarterback had an excellent reputation as a passer and had a quick delivery time—which meant that the Eagle squad must get to the passer in record time and make an impression as the quarterback was taken down. He wanted to devote this practice session to the procedures used in rushing the passer. The red squad was assigned the duty of representing the Comanche Gap team with Emmitt Wilson as the quarterback. As the practice progressed, Coach Havens took a position inside the defensive huddle of the Eagle team (the blue squad). He commented to the huddle that the key to their success was the interruption of the Comanche passing game—the key to the Eagles winning the game. The Eagles were defending pass play after pass play with a critique from the coach after each play with evaluation directed at selected team members. As the practice continued, Emmitt was able to complete a good percent of his passes causing Coach Havens to raise his voice and demand a stronger performance in rushing the passer.

Finally, anyone standing near the huddle could hear Coach Havens say in a stern voice, "Dammit! Take him out! Hurt him! To win you must destroy the passer's ability to complete passes!"

"But coach, this passer is one of us! We don't want to injure him!" said Josh Ford, a defensive lineman.

"No! Dammit! He is not one of us! He represents our opponent—Comanche Gap! Take him out! Forget the identity of the passer! He is trying to beat us with his passes! Just remember that he is trying to defeat us!" stormed the coach.

THE SECOND INJURY

Another pass play was run. Wilson completed the pass some 40-yards down the field. Coach Havens talked individually to each member of the defensive line each with a described defensive assignment. The next play was called. The defensive line plus two linebacks charged with renewed vigor. Three linemen broke through the offensive line followed by one linebacker. They seemed to reach Wilson at almost the same time. Wilson was tackled by the two linemen—one from each side—followed by the linebackers. There was a pileup of the defensive and offensive players. The whistle blew, and the players began to free themselves from the pile—all but Wilson who remained motionless on the ground. One of the Eagle players motioned for the coach to come to the injured player. Soon two assistant coaches rushed to look at Emmitt.

Coach Gilmore shouted to Havens, "Coach, you need to take a look at this!"

Coach Havens replied, "He'll be all right. Let Parker take over as quarterback."

"No! Coach, Emmitt is hurt bad!"

Havens came to Emmitt's prone body, knelt down beside him, and after a brief observation said, "Call the doctor!"

READER PLEASE NOTE:

The story up to this point has been a review of events following the first injury of Emmitt Wilson—from this point forward is an account of what happened after the second injury.

BLUEFIELD EAGLES
THE EIGHTH GAME OF THE SEASON: COMANCHE GAP
OCTOBER 29TH

As predicted, Comanche Gap showed every indication of a determined and effective passing game, whereas—as one of the Bluefield coaches commented—the Bluefield Eagles did not seem to have their heart in the game. Even though the Bluefield Eagles had practiced long and hard concerning rushing the passer, their rush lacked the determination needed to reach the passer and disrupt the passing process. At the half, Comanche led by a score of 20 to 3. Bluefield had been able to gain yardage with short passes often to fifteen and—at times—twenty yards but had been unable to mount a single serious scoring threat.

As the second half got underway, it seemed obvious that Bluefield would have to rely on a ground attack to take the game back from Comanche Gap. During the third quarter, Bluefield was able to score a field goal while Comanche Gap scored two touchdowns—one by passing and the second by a ground attack.

The fourth quarter was much of the same type of offense by each team. Comanche Gap scored a field goal midway through the quarter. Bluefield managed a field goal with seven minutes remaining in the game. As the game progressed, Bluefield scored a touchdown as the clock ran out, and the game ended with a score of Comanche Gap 34 and Bluefield 19.

THE NATIONAL NEWS SERVICE
SPORTS REVIEW

by

HERB GORMLEY

A multitude of events have transpired since my last column regarding the football program at Bluefield University. The third-team quarterback was severely injured in a team practice session on Wednesday of last week. The team was involved in a scrimmage preparation for a scheduled game with Comanche Gap.

The Bluefield University coaching staff had expressed concern regarding the effectiveness of the Comanche Gap quarterback and his ability as a passer. Therefore, the Wednesday scrimmage was designed to emphasize the need for a strong defense by the Bluefield team. Thus, third-string quarterback Emmitt Wilson was to simulate the Comanche Gap quarterback and his passing ability. The reason given for this change was that the Bluefield third-string quarterback was a better passer than the second-team quarterback. The entire scrimmage was evidently designed to emphasize to the Bluefield team the importance of disrupting the passing attack by Comanche Gap. This was done midway through the practice when two Bluefield chargers approached the third team quarterback and delivered blows on each side of his helmet which caused an injury so severe that it required hospital confinement.

The injured quarterback was unconscious for a day and a half with a concussion and then came in and out of consciousness for another day. Recovery has not progressed as expected, and Wilson is still confined to the Regional Hospital with the latest diagnosis stating that he is now suffering from bleeding in the brain area. Brain bleeding is a new diagnosis and in this case is caused by pressure on the brain. If third-team quarterback Emmitt Wilson is not soon able to return to the playing field, sports in this nation will lose the exciting performance of a quality athlete.

This reporter has wondered why a player with the talents of Emmitt Wilson has not been placed above the third-team on the team's position chart. Even though he has only played quarterback in seven games this season for a total of thirty-seven minutes and seven seconds of playing time, he has thrown three 100-yard passes, plus two eighty-three-yard passes, and one sixty-yard pass. It seems he has only been used when one of the other quarterbacks has been injured or when winning the game was in doubt.

When I asked the coach for an explanation, I was told that because of his limited six-man team experience in high school, he was not of the same caliber as the other two quarterbacks. In my opinion, that was a true statement. He certainly is not of the same caliber—he is far above them, especially in his passing ability. I have always believed that a coach's responsibility was to train his team touching on every position, to select the most talented players for each position, and build his coaching strategy around the results. As a sports reporter, I am among the first to believe that a coach must be the one to make the decisions concerning his team, but I also believe that as a sports fan, one has the right to ask for an explanation as to why certain decisions were made.

It is true that certain coaches do not place as much emphasis on the passing game as other coaches do. However, that is normally dependent on the quality of the passing ability of the team members at the time such a decision is made.

Football has a fascinating history as the sport moved from sandlot to high school to college and on to the professional leagues. During the late 1930's, as a quarterback Sammy Baugh received a great deal of notoriety for his passing ability. During his college years, he played for Texas Christian University in Texas where he was named an All-American quarterback. After completing college, he joined the Washington Redskins professional team. With his success came an interest in his background and details of his early years.

Many stories were written about his climb to fame through his passing ability. One story was how he had practiced as a teenager to perfect his passing skills. He had taken an old automobile tire, tied a rope around the tire, then tied the rope to an overhanging tree limb. He practiced throwing the football through the opening of the tire. He practiced from different distances and finally had the tire moving from side to side as he passed the ball through the opening.

Another story was that during the World War II years, in order to be exempt from the draft, he would work on his father's ranch during the week and fly to Washington on Saturday in order to practice with the team and play in the game on Sunday—returning to the Texas ranch on Sunday night.

Another story concerned the protection the team gave to Baugh when he was executing a pass play. In those days, the playing field was not always covered with grass which meant the field could be muddy in places. Baugh often played on such fields—when the game ended, the team members were often covered in mud—but Baugh would only show mud from the knees down. The explanation was that the coaches had instructed the team to protect Baugh at any cost. He was not to be taken down; therefore, the team would often take the fifteen-yard penalty but not risk Baugh being downed or injured.

So goes some of the rich history of the great sport of football.

A mind once stretched by a new idea never regains its original dimensions.

Oliver Wendell Holmes

CHAPTER NINE

WAYWARD WINDS OF A PROFESSION

CHAPTER NINE

1. Board's Discussion with Coach Havens

2. Board's List of Concerns

3. A Discussion with the Board's Attorney

4. Meeting with Coach Havens

5. Dr. Albright's Report on Wilson's Condition

6. Gormley's Sports Column

WAYWARD WINDS OF A PROFESSION

President Dr. Bowen—"I call the meeting to order. The purpose of this executive session is to again visit with Coach Havens."

Chairman Peebles—"Coach Havens, the regents are concerned about some of the events which have transpired before, during, and since Wednesday's practice. I have encouraged Board members to ask any questions which might be of concern to them. But first, I have a question. What has been your relationship with Emmitt Wilson over the past two years and especially this season?"

Coach Havens—"His freshman year, he was a walk-on and assigned to a defensive position. His second year was about the same. He did not stand out in the group. This year, he did ask for a chance to try out for the quarterback position which we did give him. Because we already had two quarterbacks in the squad, we assigned him to the gray team."

Chairman Peebles—"The gray team? That is the third team, I believe?"

Coach Havens—"Yes, that is correct."

Spurlock—"Coach Havens, is it true that you did not know his name until this incident happened?"

Coach Havens—"Of course not! I know all the squad members by name! I may not always call them by their real name. I often refer to them as any nickname they may have acquired or as to the position they play. But I know all their names."

Spurlock—"Coach, some of the coaching staff as well as some of the players have commented that you have referred to Wilson as 'What's his name' or 'the third-team quarterback.'"

Coach Havens—"Well, it may have been during a time when I could not call his name in an excitable moment, but at other times—I know his position."

McCorcle—"Coach, what is your opinion of 6-man football?"

Coach Havens—"I don't see much relation to eleven-man football. Six-man is wide open—requires more running and passing and open field blocking and tackling than eleven-man does. I have compared it to the child's game of running base."

McCorcle—"Well, coach, it seems to have prepared Wilson for the eleven-man game rather well."

Coach Havens—"I have heard that before. Some people compare a third-string quarterback who has played no more than five minutes in any game to a first-string quarterback who has played and had the responsibility to direct the team for fifty or sixty minutes or so in many games."

Spurlock—"Well, coach, that third-team quarterback you have reference to has won three games with his six-man experience and has scored 36 other points besides three touchdowns."

Coach Havens—"I know he has had lucky turnovers in his quarterback duties. But you must consider a person who has brought the team to what it is—on the verge of winning the conference championship for the third time."

Spurlock—"Coach, I am sure you are aware of the scuttlebutt going around that you may have an ulterior motive for ignoring Wilson."

Coach Havens—"I maintain the fact that I have placed the players with the most experience in any key position!"

Spurlock—"Are you saying that experience can replace talent?"

Coach Havens—"No! But at times, talent can only be displayed when certain conditions exist and is not always used for the welfare of the team."

Spurlock—"Coach, I understand your gift of $30,000 did not win you any friends in your coaching staff nor in the team personnel."

Coach Havens—"I resent your reference to the gift that you refer to! I consider that a reward for the time and effort I have given the son of the parent who gave the gift!"

McCorcle—"Coach, have you received any other gifts from team parents?"

Coach Havens—"I resent this line of questioning! The gift was perfectly legal, and I do not intend to discuss it anymore!"

Chairman Peebles—"You are not at liberty to determine the Regents' line of questioning! I suggest you take advantage of this opportunity given to you to explain some of your questionable activities!"

Coach Havens—"Yes, sir. I apologize."

Chairman Peebles—"Regents, let's continue with our questions."

Hernandez—"Coach, from your response to our questions today, you don't seem to think much of Wilson. At least in my opinion, you do not give him much if any credit for his performance this year. Do you dislike the boy for some reason?"

Coach Havens—"Oh! I give him credit. I just doubt that he has proven himself in my opinion."

McCorcle—"How can he prove himself if he isn't allowed to play?"

Chairman Peebles—"Then coach, it seems that you feel our first- and second- team quarterbacks are better qualified than Wilson at playing eleven-man football?"

Coach Havens—"Oh yes—by far!"

Chairman Peebles—"Is your opinion based solely on his experience in six-man football?"

Coach Havens—"Yes, it is!"

Claude—"Then why was he recruited?"

Coach Havens—"He was not recruited. He was a walk-on."

Chairman Peebles—"You mean he just showed up on the first day of practice three years ago and has been here ever since?"

Coach Havens—"Yes, that is true."

McCorcle—"Then why was he given a scholarship?"

Coach Havens—"He was not given a scholarship."

McCorcle—"He still does not have one after three years on the team?"

Coach Havens—"No, he does not."

Spurlock—"What would it take for him to be placed on a scholarship?"

Coach Havens—"We would need to wait until next year. All the scholarship positions are filled at this time."

Spurlock—"Do you mean to say that even with his demonstrated passing ability he could not be placed on a scholarship at this time?"

Coach Havens—"All scholarships which we are eligible for have already been awarded."

Chairman Peebles—"If our first-and second-team quarterbacks are so good, why was Wilson given the passing assignment for Comanche Gap during the scrimmage?"

Coach Havens—"We thought his passing ability could demonstrate the efficiency of the regular Comanche Gap quarterback."

Williams—"Does this mean he's good enough for practice but not for games?"

McCorcle—"Coach, I realize you have been pushing Gray into the selection by a professional team, and I understand your actions there. That is well and good. But are you afraid of Wilson overshadowing Gray?"

Coach Havens—"No! Certainly not! Gray—through three years of excellent team leadership—has earned the right to lead this team."

McCorcle—"I am not talking about leading the team. I am just asking about him throwing passes which have led us to victory at least three times so far this year."

Coach Havens—"Wilson does make a contribution to the game with his passing."

Chairman Peebles—"We will adjourn this meeting at this time since the Board has another meeting scheduled within the hour."

Before scheduling another meeting with Coach Havens, the Board of Regents had a conference with several members of the coaching staff as well as three members of the football team. During these conferences, the Board attempted to ascertain the feelings of the person being interviewed. These conferences caused the Board to have a deeper concern regarding the head coach's supervision and management of the football program. Even with the feedback from the eight individual conferences with assistant coaches and team members, the mystery still remained as to the relationship between coach Havens and team member Emmitt Wilson. Four of the coaches interviewed expressed the belief that the head coach has the authority to dictate any phase of the football program to his prescribed method of approaching any part of the football program.

Attorney Woods—"Then why have assistant coaches?"

Coach Arnold—"To carry out the head coach's philosophy and directions."

The conference session with each coach seemed to indicate that Wilson's passing ability was outstanding and that his attitude was wholesome in spite of the fact that the head coach never indicated any recognition of that ability. Havens on several occasions referred to Wilson as "What's his name." The team players readily recognized Wilson's passing ability as well as his knowledge of the game. Three of the coaches seemed to feel that Coach Havens had the authority to do as he deemed advisable in dealing with Wilson. The other three assistant coaches expressed concern over the way Wilson was treated. Each of the team members was complimentary of Wilson's attitude—stating that they had never heard Wilson complain or "badmouth" any member of the coaching staff.

The coaching staff refused to compare the first-team quarterback—Jeff Gray—and Wilson other than to say that Wilson's passing had been outstanding even though his playing time in any given game had been limited to only a few minutes.

At 9:00 the next morning, the Board of Regents assembled in the University Executive Conference Room with all members present along with Attorney Woods and University President Dr. Donald Bowen.

Spurlock—"I cannot believe what has been done to that boy!"

Ford—"And all from one person's greed!"

Cloud—"Let's list our concerns about Havens."

Chairman Peebles—"Good idea! Who wants to start the list?"

BOARD'S LIST OF CONCERNS

As the meeting progressed, a list of concerns was formulated which included the following:

1. Accepting two "gift" payments from a player's parent
2. Downplaying the six-man football experience
3. Failing to recognize Wilson's ability
4. Limiting Wilson's playing time in games this season
5. Placing Wilson on the scrimmage team representing Comanche Gap
6. Lacking concern at the time of Wilson's injury
7. Downplaying Wilson's injury even at the hospital

Chairman Peebles—"We will now go into a discussion of the concerns we have listed. As we progress, if you think of other concerns, they can be added to the list."

Chairman Peebles—"Attorney Woods, would you care to comment on the items listed?"

Attorney Woods—"Yes, I have noted the items listed. Some I note you are dissatisfied with or do not agree with, but they are not items which you have the authority to change. Let's look at each item.

1. Accepting gifts from a parent is not illegal. The coach has a perfect right to accept gifts. It may not be a wise thing to do on his part, but the accepting itself is not illegal.

2. Downplaying six-man football is simply using his right to express his opinion. Again, this may not have been a wise thing to do under the circumstances, but it is not illegal.

3. Failing to recognize Wilson's ability is perhaps poor coaching, but it falls under the duties he is paid to do. Again, nothing illegal.

4. Limiting Wilson's playing time in games is also one of the duties he is paid to do, wise or unwise.

5. Placing Wilson in the scrimmage representing Comanche Gap is also one of his duties. However, this may be the strongest point of your concern. If we can show that Havens placed Wilson in harm's way for a selfish purpose, then we have a very strong point.

6. Havens' lack of concern when it was obvious that Wilson was injured was also not illegal—poor judgement and poor coaching, but not illegal.

7. Downplaying Wilson's injury even at the hospital

was again just his opinion. Not very smart, but not illegal."

Spurlock—"Mark, are you indicating that the University does not have much of a case as to removing Havens from his coaching position?"

Chairman Peebles—"Surely the coach is not at liberty to make such decisions and leave the Board powerless to correct such a situation!"

Attorney Woods—"I would suggest we redirect our approach to the situation. For example:

1. Expose the reasons for the gift.
2. Show how the gifts have influenced Havens' decisions.
3. Show how Havens' fear of Wilson overshadowing Gray and why it affected his actions.
4. Dwell on Havens deliberately placing Wilson in a position to suffer an injury, especially the nonuse of the red quarterback jacket for one thing.

Even with all of the items just mentioned, the Regents' strongest point for removing Havens from his current position and his most motivating factor will be the damage such exposure will do to his career."

Williams—"Mark, why do you say that?"

Attorney Woods—"Wherever he would go, recruiting would be a stumbling block. Few places would employ a coach with a record of sacrificing a player for selfish reasons much less deliberately trying to get a player hurt, and few players would be willing to play for such a coach."

Chairman Peebles—"Then we need to reorganize our approach to the matter."

Attorney Woods—"Yes, that is the next step. Keep in mind, as the situation gets more exposure in the news and individual conversations, some of the coaching staff will attempt to defend Havens and the actions he has taken. Some others will not be supportive in a subtle way or will take a 'middle of the road' stand. When or if you become involved in such a conversation, I suggest you concentrate on listening and not on arguing different points. If the news media presents the facts in a fair and just manner, it will be one of the strong points in our case."

At the scheduled day and time, members of the Board of Regents met in the University conference room with Coach Havens for a third time.

Chairman Peebles called the meeting to order and stated that the purpose of this called meeting was to "make additional inquiries into the events leading up to the scrimmage in which Emmitt Wilson was injured and the developments which have occurred beyond the day of the scrimmage."

Chairman Peebles—"Coach Havens, as you have been advised, we desire to look further into the events leading up to and beyond the scrimmage in which Emmitt Wilson was injured. The Board has questions concerning several past developments."

Spurlock—"Coach, I understand that since Wilson was injured, he has asked you why you 'dislike him so much.' Is that true?"

Coach Havens—"Yes, it is! It stunned me when he asked that question. I certainly do not dislike any of the players on our team and surely not Wilson. I cannot fathom what prompted such a question."

Hernandez—"Do you have a problem with his name? They tell me you have referred to him on a number of occasions as 'what's his name.' After all, this is his third year as a member of the team."

Coach Havens—"I explained to Emmitt that there are times during the excitement of a practice or a game when I sometimes refer to a player by the position he plays. It is not that I don't know the player's name."

Claude—"Coach, I have wondered why with Emmitt's ability he does not get to play more. I am not trying to run your coaching job. But I have been asked this same question a number of times."

Coach Havens—"Well, I can answer that question! Jeff Gray is the number one quarterback of our team. He has had that assignment going on his third year. He has done well—we won the conference championship with his direction last year. He is leading well this year. Wilson is like a flash in the pan—he has only played a limited amount of time. Emmitt's pass receivers deserve a great deal of credit for catching his passes. I feel you forget the leadership that Gray has provided and are giving extra credit to Wilson for limited passing performance."

McCorcle—"Coach, during the scrimmage in question, if you had our second team representing Comanche Gap, why was Emmitt Wilson put in as their quarterback instead of Dick Parker? He is the assigned quarterback for that team, is he not?"

Coach Havens—"Yes, he is. But Wilson is a better passer than Parker."

Chairman Peebles—"Mr. Havens, our athletic department is going to have a hard time 'living down' the statements you made during the scrimmage. I refer to 'take him out of there' and 'hurt him!'"

Coach Havens—"I am sorry for my excited outburst, but I was emotionally involved in the practice."

Chairman Peebles—"We will be trying to explain that for years to come. But now our paramount concern is Wilson's recovery. The doctors have given us little encouragement concerning his full recovery."

Dr. Cowan—"The primary concern as of now is that Wilson lapses into unconsciousness usually at least once each day. He now remains so for a period of four to six hours. I have no medical explanation for these occurrences. I am calling in a specialist from Kansas City who works with professional teams regarding head injuries. His name is Dr. William Albright. You may have seen his name mentioned in the sports pages."

Chairman Peebles—"When do you expect him to arrive?"

Dr. Cowan—"He should arrive tonight. He wants to observe Wilson before, during, and after he loses consciousness. Since Wilson normally passes out during the early afternoon, Dr, Albright hopes to complete his examination all in one day."

Dr. Albright did arrive at the expected time and was able to make the planned observations and have a lengthy dialogue with Wilson. At 6:00 p.m., the Board of Regents assembled to listen to Dr. Albright's report.

Dr. Albright—"Members of the Board of Regents, I have completed my observation of Emmitt Wilson. I have never been exposed to an injury with this type of results. I examined Wilson as planned before, during, and after his lapse into unconsciousness. I have no explanation for the cause of the blackouts. Unconsciousness usually follows a blow of some kind. But, of course, as I observed, there was no blow immediately preceding his unconsciousness. I will research further into this type of response, but I am at a loss at this point. I have cautioned Wilson and his athletic director that any type of brain injury causes a delicate situation which can undergo a radical change which may be followed by any number of situations. For example, any high excitement, a fall of any type, or extra effort causing rapid breathing may trigger a change regarding the brain. I will keep in touch with your athletic director and hope to find an explanation for this condition."

Chairman Peebles—"Dr. Albright, thank you for coming and examining Wilson. Be advised that your frank opinion is meaningful to us all, and it will help us in our determination of further actions.

Dr. Albright—"It is an unusual injury, and complications are difficult to pinpoint in the long run—but you have done well so far. I will be interested in any improvements that surface as well as the welfare of Wilson as time moves along."

THE NATIONAL NEWS SERVICE
SPORTS REVIEW

by

HERB GORMLEY

A FALL FROM FAVOR

When Coach Havens and his staff arrived at Bluefield University almost five years ago, they made a very favorable impression on the University staff and the administration as well as the community. They were friendly, took an active interest in community affairs, were active the the church of their choice, and displayed an interest in the high school athletic program.

This display of active interest continued up until the beginning of the current academic school year. Wilson had been an active member of the football squad since his freshman year although he had been practically ignored as far as actively participating in scheduled practice sessions—let alone in games. Wilson was well-known for his record in Sparta's six-man football program. However, Coach Havens gave little if any recognition of his athletic ability, referring to him as "what's his name" when talking to the coaching staff.

Even after Wilson was given an opportunity to demonstrate his passing skill, Coach Havens downplayed the 100-yard pass with comments of "lucky" or "the completion was because receivers had to move under his thrown passes." The news media became aware of the situation, and Coach Havens' public relations began to decline.

The limited playing time given Wilson and especially his successes were noted by sports fans, the administration, and his teammates. Still Havens was reluctant to give credit for Wilson's passing skill which resulted in his playing time being limited to 37 minutes in the seven games played before his injury.

Wilson was not available to send in to rescue his team during the Comanche Gap game. He had been sent into the scheduled game during the last few minutes of the fourth quarter to salvage the game during the last three games. He was not available this time due to his practice-related injury—thus, the game was lost. He is in the hospital fighting for his survival.

This columnist wishes him well with all of God's speed in his recovery.

I have never killed anyone, but I have read some obituary notices with great satisfaction.

Scope Trial

CHAPTER TEN

WAYWARD WINDS OF A PROFESSION

CHAPTER TEN

1. Introduction of Coach Havens' Attorney

2. Administrative Planning

3. Havens and his Attorney

4. Game Number Nine

5. Havens' Attorney Meets with Select Group

6. Meeting of the Coaching Staff

WAYWARD WINDS OF A PROFESSION

Coach Havens called President Dr. Bowen and asked if he and his attorney could schedule a conference with Dr. Bowen and the University attorney. A meeting was arranged. Havens had asked for the meeting to include the Board of Regents, but Dr. Bowen suggested that the meeting be restricted to himself and the University attorney.

In the meantime, Dr. Bowen called chairman Lee Peebles to inform him of the meeting and stated that he would advise him of the details as soon as possible.

At the scheduled time, Coach Havens and his attorney arrived at the president's office. Walker Duncan was introduced as Havens' attorney. After introductions were made and a brief review of the background events was given, Coach Havens stated that his purpose in having this meeting was to introduce his attorney as well as to clear up some of the future actions to be taken on his behalf.

Attorney Duncan—"Our contention is first of all the action of Marvin Gray in making monetary gifts to Coach Havens was not illegal and should not be a point of contention. Furthermore, Coach Havens has a three-year contract with the University as head football coach and that this is only the first year of that contract. As head coach, it was within his authority to call the plays and use the players in the positions of his professional choice. The coaching staff considers the injury to the player (a pause in naming the player is interrupted by attorney Woods to say 'He is referred to as 'what's his name' by some of the coaching staff')

President Dr. Bowen—"Mr. Duncan, the University as well as the members of the Board of Regents are well aware of the details as you have presented them."

Attorney Duncan—"Yes. I surmised as much but wish to go on record again as having stated the facts which are a matter of record."

Attorney Woods—"Mr. Duncan, you have stated the facts as the University understands them. However, the interpretation of said facts may be viewed from a different vantage point by the University."

Attorney Duncan—"Yes! I am well aware of the details as you have stated. My purpose in this meeting is to share some details which might forgo possible legal and court action."

Attorney Woods—"We appreciate your position."

Attorney Duncan—"Could I ask if you are contemplating any action at this time concerning Coach Havens?"

President Dr. Bowen—"The Board of Regents has not made any decisions as yet in regards to any action."

There being no further comments by either party, the meeting was adjourned after which President Dr. Bowen called chairman Peebles to inform him of the details of the meeting.

The following day, President Dr. Bowen assembled four members of the Board whom he considered to be key personnel involved in the athletic problem at hand. They were the chairman of the Board of Regents, Lee Peebles; the University attorney, Mark Woods; the Dean of Students, Woodrow Young; and the Athletic Director, Leo Sims. His purpose was to use a "think tank" approach in addressing the possible legal situation which seemed to be forthcoming.

President Dr. Bowen—"I encourage an open discussion concerning our approach in meeting a possible lawsuit. I feel sure Coach Havens will bring legal action into being in the event we terminate his service with the University. In fact, he may do so even if we do not take such action. Mark, as University attorney, what are your thoughts on the situation?"

Attorney Woods—"Yes! I think we are headed to a period of legal action. Even if we do not terminate his services, there is every indication that he will claim damage to his reputation as a head coach. Which is certainly true. His reputation is damaged and will continue to suffer even if he should win his case against the University."

Chairman Peebles—"It is hard for me to conceive of him winning this case."

President Dr. Bowen—"Yes! I agree; however, I want us to consider all likelihoods in our meeting today."

Athletic Director Sims—"The coaching staff feels the situation has gone beyond the point of recovery. They see the treatment he used in dealing with Emmitt Wilson as inexcusable. They are trying to stay loyal to Coach Havens, but they are losing much of their confidence in him."

Dean Young—"Even the student body is up in arms and feels that a great injustice has been done to Wilson. And if Wilson does not recover—well, I would hate to be Coach Havens!"

Dean Young continues—"I am presenting each of you with a copy of an email that members of the Student

Council forwarded to Coach Havens. Please see if you have any comments."

OPEN EMAIL TO COACH HAVENS WITH COPY TO BOARD OF REGENTS

Coach Havens,

We have a question for you: Is the treatment you are directing to Emmitt Wilson worth the damage it is reflecting on your coaching reputation?

Signed,

Members of the Student Body

All members of the Board read the email.

President Dr. Bowen—"This could be the beginning of a very unhealthy development."

Attorney Woods—"Oh! What you say is so true! If the officers of the student body are involved in sending this email, it would be hard to advise them—let alone—influence their actions."

Athletic Director Sims—"I was in hopes that we could get this issue settled without student involvement!"

Dean Young—"Three members of the Student Council brought me the email less than two hours ago!"

President Dr. Bowen—"Well, we all seem to have the same feelings about how Emmitt has been treated. But let's get down to the nitty- gritty actions of what we must do now."

Attorney Woods—"Even if they request legal action, there will be an extended period of time before the case goes to trial. For example, the two attorneys involved will employ other legal members for research and the planned legal maneuvers before and during the trial."

President Dr. Bowen—"It seems such maneuvers and actions could take months."

Attorney Woods—"Our best plan is as the two sides meet, to convince Havens that any legal action on his part does damage to his coaching reputation and may damage his chances of future employment."

Athletic Director Sims—"This may not be an effective approach in the beginning of negotiations. He has commented openly concerning his success at Bluefield and has indicated that he has had several offers to move to a larger university system because of this success at Bluefield."

President Dr. Bowen—"This is good to review past events and predictions of the future—but what are our avenues of approach for the immediate future—I am talking about tomorrow and the day after. What is our next move?"

Attorney Woods—"In our planning, I think we must assume that Havens will bring legal action concerning his termination of coaching services to Bluefield University. He will site his past coaching successes and site that in the past his relationships with the administration, the alumni, the coaching staff, and the student body have been pleasant and rewarding. He will bring proof that this has been the case. Assistant coaches will testify that the relationships have proven pleasant and satisfactory as well as rewarding."

President Dr. Bowen—"Well, so far, all I have heard is a positive review of Havens' conduct and his performance of his job description; surely, we are not going to base our termination action on such a review."

Attorney Woods—"Certainly not! This review is looking at both sides of the information that will be presented to a jury. Our side is yet to be illuminated."

Athletic Director Sims—"Our review will be different and, I believe, effective. A number of the coach's actions present a direct violation of coaching ethics, the welfare of student personnel, and the projection of the public image of the University."

Dean Young—"Let's stipulate here and now some of the Board's concerns which we will present once the trial gets underway."

Chairman Peebles—"Good idea! Who will be the first to begin the list?"

Attorney Woods—"I feel that our approach should center around items we have discussed before and are vital to this situation which are:

1. Expose the reason for the gift of $30,000.

2. Show how the gifts have influenced Havens' decisions.

3. Stress Havens' fears of Wilson overshadowing Gray.

4. Tie the overshadowing into Wilson's injury.

5. Stress the injury to Wilson.

6. Bring into the testimonies the damage Havens' career will suffer."

Athletic Director Sims—"Should we consider requesting a bench trial rather than a trial by jury?"

Attorney Woods—"We could make such a request; however, the danger might be if the judge assigned to the case was not a sports fan, he might be prone to side with the 'underdog' which would be the individual bringing the suit. Havens' lawyer might make such a request."

Chairman Peebles—"Would requesting a change of venue help our case?"

Attorney Woods—"That is something to consider because this is a college town and Havens' problems have not been widespread beyond this town. I would imagine Havens with his winning record here at Bluefield has a large number of backers locally."

Dean Young—"On the other hand, Emmitt Wilson is a sports hero who has been mistreated by Coach Havens. He has a huge number of fans who—I would think—will support him with enthusiasm no matter where the venue would be established."

Attorney Woods—"You have a point there."

President Dr. Bowen—"I think our discussion during this meeting has been meaningful and should provide Mr. Woods with an indication of the direction we would like to proceed."

President Dr. Bowen—"Before we close this meeting, does anyone have a statement they would like to make? There being none, this meeting is now closed."

BLUEFIELD EAGLES
THE NINTH GAME OF THE SEASON: THE COASTAL UNIVERSITY
NOVEMBER 5TH

The Bluefield team was a dispirited group after their defeat by Comanche Gap. They next turned their attention to game number nine against the Coastal University. Scouting reports on this next opponent was the focus of the game preparations for the next week. The Coastal team presented an effective running game with a moderate passing attack.

Each team had scored a touchdown during the first half, and the scoreboard showed a tie of 7 and 7 at halftime. The second half got underway as Coastal marched down the field to score followed by another touchdown late in the third quarter. The third quarter ended with the score of Coastal 21 and Bluefield University 10. During the balance of the fourth quarter, Bluefield University scored a field goal while Coastal also scored a field goal followed by a touchdown late in the fourth quarter. The game ended with a score of Coastal 24 and Bluefield University 13.

After Coach Havens and his attorney Walter Duncan had left the meeting with Dr. Bowen, they decided to plan a strategy meeting to be initiated in the event that Bluefield followed through with any plans to terminate the coach's contract. Based on events during the last week and specifically as an indication of the meeting with Dr. Bowen, they felt there was a strong possibility of such action by the University.

They scheduled a meeting on the following day and invited a select group to attend. The Athletic Director Leo Sims was invited; however, he declined saying if the University chose to take any legal action, he would be involved as a member of the University administration. First assistant coach Gilmore along with passing coach Johnny Cloud, offensive coordinator Jack Arnold, and backfield coach Jim Daniels were included on the invited list. The team doctor was also invited; however, he also declined due to his position with the University.

They met in the office of attorney Walter Duncan. At the very beginning of the meeting, Coach Havens stated that if any action were taken by the University, he would contest the decision to the very end. He further stated that he felt he would have strong support from the University alumni as well as from the University fans. He had a winning record from his first two years as the University coach as well as the current year. He stated that 95% of the possible charges against him really involved coaching decisions which were his duty to make—even if the administration did not agree with these decisions. He repeated that injuries were an accepted result of any football program.

Attorney Duncan—"I concur with what Coach Havens has stated. I suggest we turn our attention to projecting the items the administration will likely use as the reasons for termination action."

After a discussion and an exchange of ideas, the following list was produced:

*acceptance of the gift

*the false statement about the source of the money

*Wilson's limited playing time

*Wilson's "outlaw" practice sessions

*placing Wilson in harm's way

*saying to "hurt him!"

Attorney Duncan—"Frankly, I think Coach Havens has a very strong defense of his decisions and actions. Look at our list:

*the gift—not illegal

*the false statement—Havens was not under oath

*Wilson's limited playing time—it is the coach's job to select players for designated positions

*the 'outlaw' practice sessions—not illegal

*putting Wilson in harm's way—any player who was assigned the quarterback position on a team defending against the practice of taking out the passer would be in harm's way

*the statement supposedly made by Coach Havens during the scrimmage—'take him out of there! Hurt him!'—Coach Havens says he knows what he said and denies making such a statement."

Attorney Duncan—"I don't mean to play down the seriousness of the situation we are involved in, but to look on the bright side of our problem—we might turn our attention to how much Coach Havens wants to name as damages in his lawsuit!"

There were some smiles and moderate laughter following Duncan's statement.

Coach Havens—"The thought has crossed my mind!"

Attorney Duncan—"However, the reality of any court case should be a vital concern to this group. I ask you to pay strict attention to the word damages. The longer the news coverage about the injured student stays before the public, the greater damage to Coach Havens' reputation. News items in print—whether true or false—can greatly influence the public."

Attorney Duncan—"I can imagine the long list of items Bluefield will present as reasons for terminating Havens' contract—I also believe that possibly 90% of those items fall under the duties of a coach in fulfilling his contract. My professional opinion is that they will concentrate on these items:

*accepting the gift

*the false statement

*the coach's statement about 'hurt him!'

*putting a player in harm's way.

Any university hiring a head coach would be concerned about an applicant having any of these items on his record. However, I am led to believe that the next step in this scenario will be a meeting of the two lawyers—Woods and myself—to agree on general procedures to be followed by the two lawyers involved. So we are at a standstill until we get more directions regarding the legal procedures."

THE MEETING OF THE COACHING STAFF

Leo Sims, Athletic Director of the University, called a meeting of the entire coaching staff.

Athletic Director Sims—"Staff members, I have called this meeting to brief you on the events that have taken place regarding the scrimmage that took place on Wednesday as well as to project the future chain of events."

Coach Havens—"It is important that you know the details of the developments that have taken place. Please give us your full attention."

Athletic Director Sims—"Once you have been briefed, you will be given the opportunity to ask questions and make comments."

Gilmore—"Leo, we appreciate this meeting."

Athletic Director Sims—"As you are aware, the chain of events which followed Wednesday's scrimmage and Emmitt Wilson's injury have triggered a serious situation. Not only the news media but also the Board of Regents have taken steps which place the University, the coaching staff, and the administration in a position of defending our actions and comments up to this point. Coach Havens has been placed in the position of defending the non-use of the red jacket normally used in a scrimmage. Marvin Gray, father of the first team quarterback, has come forward to say he was the individual who made financial gifts to Coach Havens. Though not considered illegal, this will be most difficult to defend."

Coach Havens—"Let me interrupt to say I was wrong in accepting the two monetary gifts, but this is water under the bridge at this time."

Athletic Director Sims—"As you have been able to observe in the sports news coverage of the scrimmage, it even quoted comments Coach Havens supposedly made during the scrimmage."

Coach Havens—"I have certainly been placed on the defensive."

Athletic Director Sims—"The tone of the meetings conducted by the Board of Regents is not good. I can't go further into the details of the meetings, but I have been included in certain parts of these meetings."

Gilmore—"Be honest! Where could this situation lead to?"

Athletic Director Sims—"It could lead to the dismissal of part or all of the football coaching staff."

Gilmore—"How could that happen?"

Athletic Director Sims—"Most if not all of your contracts are tied to the head coach. When he leaves, you are all subject to a contract review."

Gilmore—"What is the Board's concern with Coach Havens?"

Athletic Director Sims—"The main concern is with the 'why' and 'how' of the injury to Wilson. The 'why' of Wilson's playing time is also a primary discussion item."

Daniels—"Well, some of us had nothing to do with Wilson's playing time."

Athletic Director Sims—"You are all in this together."

Carson—"What about the future?"

Coach Havens—"I am consulting an attorney to see what options are available. I will keep you informed."

Athletic Director Sims—"I suggest you go ahead with your assigned coaching duties for now."

The can opener was invented forty-eight years after the can.

Zane Tray

CHAPTER ELEVEN

WAYWARD WINDS
OF A PROFESSION

CHAPTER ELEVEN

1. Wilson's Release from the Hospital

2. Meeting of the Attorneys

3. Personnel Action

4. Havens' Termination

5. The National News Service

WAYWARD WINDS
OF A PROFESSION

EMMITT'S RELEASE FROM THE HOSPITAL

After a two-week stay in the hospital, Emmitt was released from confinement. However, he was listed as an outpatient and was to report back on a daily basis. He was instructed not to return to his job of providing janitorial services to the chemistry building. This presented no problem since members of the football team had taken turns in doing this work for him since Emmitt's confinement.

Almost immediately, Emmitt asked to go to the practice field and test his passing ability. The doctors did not sanction such an activity, but Emmitt insisted with the statement that if he could not do such an activity under the supervision of the Athletic Director, he would do it on his own.

After two days of Emmitt's insisting, the doctor finally agreed providing that the Athletic Director supervise the limited activity and it be confined to not more than a twenty-minute session. Emmitt asked that there be no spectators. However, Herb Gormley secretly observed the activity from a distance with a pair of binoculars. The group arrived at the practice field with Ellis Fry and Jim Majors who would serve as receivers in the passing exercises. The activity started with a limbering exercise followed by short passes of no more than ten yards. When the activity increased to passes of twenty yards, it was obvious that Emmitt was not comfortable as he flinched during each delivery. As the activity increased to a thirty-yard pass, Emmitt's lack of accuracy was very noticeable, and no further passes were tried.

At this point, Athletic Director Sims asked Emmitt to rest a while and began questioning Emmitt as to his reaction to the problem. Emmitt readily stated that—as he expressed it—he felt faraway thunder in his head as he released the ball on delivery. He further stated that his equilibrium was not steady as he set his feet for delivery.

Emmitt passed his performance off as perhaps he had asked for the exercise too early in his recovery. However, it was obvious to Sims that Emmitt was shaken by his reaction to his performance when tears began to form in his eyes. When Sims concluded the exercise, there was no objection from Emmitt. On the way back from the practice field, Emmitt commented that each time he threw a pass, just as he released the ball, he could feel or hear what sounded like faraway thunder. It only lasted for a brief second, but it happened each time he released the ball. His follow-up statement was, "I wonder what causes that noise?" When they returned to the campus, Dr. Cowan was waiting for them and asked that Sims and Emmitt join him in his office. Dr. Cowan asked for comments from both Emmitt and Sims. After hearing their comments, he did not seem surprised by Emmitt's remark about hearing thunder. He suggested that any further such activity be delayed to a later date. He cautioned Emmitt not to push too hard or too fast at returning to his old self.

Later, when reporting to the coaching staff, Sims stated that Emmitt was far removed from his old self. He further commented that he knew Emmitt wanted a quick recovery, but, in his opinion, it was a long way down the road.

At the same time, the two opposing attorneys met to discuss the possible future developments in the case at hand.

Attorney Duncan—"Has the Board of Regents come to any decision regarding Havens' future?"

Attorney Woods—"No formal action has been recorded; however, all discussion seems to indicate that such action will be taken in the immediate future. The Board has delayed action until the football season can be completed."

Attorney Duncan—"In the event its decision is to terminate Havens' contract, I can assure you that Havens does not plan to take such action without putting up a legal fight. Please be advised that such action would be adverse publicity for the University."

Attorney Woods—"That may be true; however, I assume you have advised Havens that—win or lose—the action will already have a damaging effect on his future reputation. Such a procedure will get state-wide attention. You can imagine how Gormley will treat the situation in his column."

Attorney Duncan—"I think Havens has contemplated all possible outcomes but is dead-set on bringing suits."

Attorney Woods—"The Board of Regents is standing by for a called meeting to discuss Havens' future. I will keep you advised of any action affecting Havens."

PERSONNEL ACTION BY THE BOARD OF REGENTS

Chairman Peebles—"Board members, this meeting has been called to take action concerning the personnel matter involving Coach Havens. We have discussed this matter on a number of occasions during the last two weeks. Attorney Woods will conduct the balance of this meeting."

Attorney Woods—"As I understand things, the purpose of our meeting is to take action on the future tenure involving Coach Havens. Am I correct in this assumption?"

Chairman Peebles—"That is the purpose of this meeting. Please proceed."

Attorney Woods—"Then first we need to determine the date for the termination to be in effect. You have the following choices:

1. immediately—on today's date

2. at the end of the current month

3. at the end of the current semester

4. at the end of the current school year

5. at the end of Havens' contract

You understand his departure from the University would be within the number of days to be determined. What you would be determining here would be the length of time he would be drawing his salary. Would you care to discuss this, or are you ready to make a determination now?"

Chairman Peebles—"We have discussed this from time to time. I think the group needs to make a choice of one of the five you have listed."

After a limited amount of discussion, it was determined that the coach would be paid through the end of the current school year.

Attorney Woods—"Very well. We need a motion and a vote on the motion."

Spurlock—"I move that Coach Havens' contract be terminated effective today's date; however, his salary will continue through the end of the current school year."

Williams—"I second the motion."

Chairman Peebles—"Are there any other motions? If not, we will proceed with the voting."

Chairman Peebles—"Your vote will be recorded by voice vote identification which is to say when your individual name is called, you will voice your vote as 'YES' or 'NO'—and the vote will be recorded as expressed. This way, each board member's individual vote will be shown in the minutes of the meeting."

Chairman Peebles continues—"The motion is to terminate Coach Havens' contract effective on today's date. However, his salary will continue through the end of the current University year. The motion has been seconded."

Chairman Peebles continues—"Any questions concerning the motion?"

Chairman Peebles—"There being none, we will proceed. As the secretary calls your name, you are to respond with a 'yes' in supporting the motion or a 'no' to indicate you are opposed to the motion. Are there any questions?"

Chairman Peebles—"There being none, we will proceed. The secretary will now call the roll."

Board Chairman Peebles— "Yes."

Vice Chairman Sam Spurlock— "Yes."

Secretary Cliff Hernandez— "Yes."

Recorder Jeff McCorcle— "Yes."

Member Ted Ford— "Yes."

Member Johnny Watson— "Yes."

Member J.L. Williams— "Yes."

Member Earl Long— "Yes."

Secretary Cliff Hernandez—"All members have voted. The record will show the motion is carried with all of the Board members voting in favor of the motion."

Chairman Peebles—"Attorney Woods, you are hereby directed to prepare all necessary paperwork to carry out the legal aspects of the motion."

Attorney Woods—"I am sure that our action today will start other 'wheels' rolling. I will keep you advised."

News of Havens' termination by the Board of Regents did not surprise the coaching staff nor the news media. Their response to the action was somewhat sullen. However, the situation had been building for several weeks. The student body was quite vocal in their expressed approval of the Board of Regents' decision.

Coach Havens' only comment to the press was "I didn't realize I had such few friends." Members of the football squad were torn between loyalty to the coach or to their team member Emmitt.

BLUEFIELD EAGLES
THE TENTH GAME OF THE SEASON: COLORADO TECH
NOVEMBER 12th

Bluefield's lineup for the last game of the season returned to the usual team leaders in their original positions. The offensive line was much the same—however, the defensive line and as well as the secondary was somewhat depleted by a lack of the original members. The team morale seemed to be at an all-time low.

Colorado Tech had presented a strong running attack all season, and, as the season progressed, a moderate passing attack had developed. At half time, Tech led by a score of 17 to 3. Tech's passing attack had gained strength as the game progressed.

During the third quarter, Bluefield was able to score a touchdown through a series of short passes while Tech scored two touchdowns using their ground game. The quarter ended with a score of Tech 31 and Bluefield 10.

The fourth quarter was much the same as Bluefield scored a touchdown and two field goals while Tech scored two touchdowns making the final score Tech 45 and Bluefield 23.

THE NATIONAL NEWS SERVICE SPORTS REVIEW

by

HERB GORMLEY

PAST HEADLINES TELL A STORY

During Emmitt Wilson's short tenure as a third-team quarterback for the Bluefield University Eagle football team, the following headlines were flashed across the sports sections of the local and state newspapers from time to time during the seven games in which he was involved.

BLUEFIELD UNIVERSITY—A 100-YARD PASS PLAY

THIRD-TEAM QUARTERBACK COMPLETES A SECOND 100-YARD PASS

QUARTERBACK WILSON DOES IT AGAIN!

WAS THIRD-TEAM QUARTERBACK SACRIFICED?

37 MINUTES PLAYING TIME IN 7 GAMES—TO FOOTBALL GLORY

Some individuals have been able to cram a number of memorable sports achievements into a career of participation in a given sport. Normally the event takes place over a number of games or even seasons. This is not true for Emmitt Wilson of the Bluefield football team. He had such a limited time to make his impact on the college sport of football. However, in a short period of time, he has set the bar for successfully completing the long distance pass at an extremely high mark.

Due to a recent injury, Emmitt has a long road to recovery. He has so much to offer the sport, and we wish him well in his road to recovery.

The government can't give to anybody anything it doesn't take from somebody else.

Ives Duncan

CHAPTER TWELVE

WAYWARD WINDS OF A PROFESSION

CHAPTER TWELVE

1. Dr. Cowan's Meeting with Emmitt and his Parents

2. Emmitt's Review of Outpatient Expectations

3. Dr. Cowan's Discussion with the Coaching Staff

4. Dr. Bowen and the Athletic Director

WAYWARD WINDS OF A PROFESSION

DR. COWAN MEETS WITH EMMITT AND HIS PARENTS

After a week of outpatient treatment where Emmitt reported to the hospital each day, Dr. Cowan changed this outpatient routine so that Emmitt would only report on a weekly basis.

Mrs. Wilson—"Dr. Cowan, has Emmitt improved enough during his outpatient time to warrant such a change?"

Dr. Cowan—"Yes! I think so. The bleeding has been stopped for a period of ten days now. Emmitt's color has improved, and he walks and maneuvers at a much-improved gait. He is not well by any means, but my diagnosis is that he is now on the road to recovery."

Mrs. Wilson—"How active can he be? You know he is sometimes hard to keep in tow."

Dr. Cowan—"Moderate activities for a while, then we should be able to progress at a more rapid pace."

Dr. Cowan—"Emmitt, keep in mind that healing from your type of injury is a slow process. Your improvement will come in stages. You will have some difficulty with motor movements; balance and gait problems are likely to occur down the road, but this is what we will turn our attention to, and improvements will occur."

Mrs. Wilson—"How long will this situation last?"

Dr. Cowan—"For some time—maybe several weeks or even months. Any kind of a blow to his head could be a serious setback; for a while, even high excitement could trigger a relapse."

The next day, Emmitt had a scheduled meeting with Dr. Cowan to initiate his weekly outpatient schedule.

Dr. Cowan—"It is good to see you again, Emmitt. I had a nice visit yesterday with you and your parents. I want to take this opportunity to talk with you privately. I did not go into much detail when visiting with you and your parents. I feel your mother has enough to be concerned about without my adding more. But Emmitt, for example, a hard blow to your head could prove to be lethal, and a high degree of excitement on your part could produce equal results. I didn't want to make such a statement to your parents. I will leave that up to you. You may quote any of our discussion today to them if you see fit. But I want you to be aware of the possible dangers you face."

Emmitt—"Dr. Cowan, how long will this condition last?"

Dr. Cowan—"It is difficult to be specific. As you recover your health, these conditions may cease to exist. Only time will tell."

Emmitt—"I had so many dreams. I wanted to get to the pros so I could earn enough to help Mom and Dad. I even wanted to buy a ranch next to their property. And boy! Did I have dreams about life once that was accomplished!"

Dr. Cowan—"I can understand, Emmitt, and I can well appreciate the dreams you had built in your mind. Have patience—time is our best ally."

Emmitt—"When will I be able to take some kind of exercise? It seems so long since I was able to run and jump rope or do some kind of activity to keep in shape."

Dr. Cowan—"Now Emmitt, don't try to rush your activities. Remember that we do not want to do anything which would cause a relapse of any kind. If you will take it slow and easy, progress will come."

Emmitt—"I know—I am just overanxious--but I am a nobody without my passing skills."

Dr. Cowan—"Your passing skills are what I am trying to protect."

Emmitt—"Thanks, Dr. Cowan."

President Dr. Bowen had requested that Dr. Cowan meet with the coaching staff to provide accurate details about Wilson's injury as well as to report any progress made since his hospitalization.

When the staff was assembled, Dr. Bowen introduced Dr. Cowan and stated his position in the Regional Hospital. He also stated that Dr. Cowan had been the attending physician since Emmitt had been admitted to the hospital.

Dr. Cowan—"Thank you, Dr. Bowen. As Dr. Bowen has stated, I have been asked to provide you with details of Emmitt's stay in the hospital. During my presentation to you, I am sure I will cover quite a bit of information which you have already been exposed to by the medics or other sources. However, Dr. Bowen has requested that I present you with the official version of events as they transpired. I will attempt to answer any questions you may have at the end of my presentation."

Dr. Cowan continued—"Wilson was received at the Regional Hospital at approximately 3:30 p.m., on Wednesday, October 25th with a severe head injury together with neck and shoulder injuries. After being unconscious for some eighteen hours, he returned to consciousness. However, every six to eight hours, he lapsed back into a state of unconsciousness for anywhere from four to six hours. This type of reaction was repeated for almost two days and nights. He has been clear of this reaction for six days as of this early a.m. His main problem developed into a period of brain bleeding. For a period of time due to continuous bleeding, we were unable to determine the exact source of the bleeding—whether the bleeding was coming from an area around the brain or coming from inside the brain. We have now determined that the source of the bleeding is a colloid cyst which is causing pressure on the brain which, as a result, is causing the brain bleeding."

Dr. Cowan continued—"His injury was primarily caused by two blows to the head at almost the same time—coming on each side of the helmet. During all of this, one of Emmitt's major concerns has been if he has missed the spring training of the football program."

Dr. Cowan—"Do you have any questions at this point?"

Gilmore—"Dr. Cowan, Emmitt seems to be taking a longer period of time to recover than most of us expected. What would be the cause of such a delay?"

Dr. Cowan—"It might seem so, but in this case, we are dealing with a very serious brain injury. The simultaneous blows to the head and the bleeding of the brain complicated our diagnosis as well as the prescribed treatment."

Arnold—"Will he be able to be involved in our spring training?"

Dr. Cowan—"That remains to be seen. As I am sure you realize, with Emmitt's passing ability and especially his long passes, with each team you play, Emmitt will be a marked man, and their defensive assignment will be to 'GET THE PASSER!' This places him in an extra-vulnerable position. Likely, without his extra passing ability, he would be just another passer, but with his extra passing talent, he is the 'bull's eye' for every defense. I would imagine that each opposing coach would stress the fact that extra effort should be put forth toward eliminating this passing threat."

Cloud—"I know when he was first injured, there was talk about a shoulder problem. What is the status of this situation?"

Dr. Cowan—"The brain injury has been our pressing concern; however, the shoulder injury has proved to be mending in an acceptable manner."

Daniels—"I know Emmitt has been placed on an outpatient status now. Is this a hopeful sign pointing to a recovery?"

Dr. Cowan—"It definitely is a step forward and a hopeful sign of recovery; however, Emmitt's complete recovery is a long way off, and he will need dedicated attention on his road to recovery."

Dr. Bowen and The Athletic Director

As the meeting adjourned, Dr. Bowen asked Leo Sims for a brief conference.

President Dr. Bowen—"Mr. Sims, this situation has all indication of possibly developing into an explosive situation. The attitude of the Board has taken a definite decline in their support for Coach Havens, and, as you are aware, the news media has a tendency of blowing events out of proportion. My purpose in visiting with you is to ask you to work with individual members of the staff and team to not be involved in passing along rumors—try to wait until things happen before speculating as to the outcome of a particular event."

Athletic Director Sims—"Yes. I realize a real problem may be just around the corner about not only Coach Havens' job security but especially their own."

President Dr. Bowen—"You realize that the longer this situation goes on, it can become a national news item which would be detrimental to the University."

Athletic Director Sims—"Yes, I realize that is a real possibility."

President Dr. Brown—"Well, I thank you for listening to me, and please do the best you can."

Athletic Director Sims—"I will give the situation my devoted attention. I think our main problem is going to be keeping Emmitt Wilson in tow. He is so anxious to recover and keep perfecting his passing skills."

President Dr. Bowen—"I know. His enthusiasm may be the breaking point of all of the recovery plans."

Athletic Director Sims—"I will talk to his mother without causing her undue concern and say something like the team is pulling for him and wants him to follow the doctor's prescribed recovery plan so he can get back to the team practices as soon as the doctor gives his o.k."

President Dr. Bowen—"That sounds like a good approach—let's try it."

Do all the good you can. By all the means you can. In all the ways you can. In all the places you can. At all the times you can. To all the people you can. As long as you can.

> John Wesley—eighteenth century theologian

CHAPTER THIRTEEN

WAYWARD WINDS OF A PROFESSION

CHAPTER THIRTEEN

1. Details Concerning an Administrative Hearing

2. The Hearing Process

3. Emmitt's Second Visit to the Practice Field

4. The Administrative Remedy Hearing

5. Follow-up from the Hearing

WAYWARD WINDS OF A PROFESSION

Attorney Woods advised the Board of a section in the University Personnel Policy Manual which stipulates that certain positions on the University Organizational Chart are allowed to request an Administrative Remedy Hearing when a personnel problem of this type develops. The position of head coach is included as a part of this policy.

Chairman Peebles—"Therefore, we will need to offer such a hearing."

Attorney Woods—"The purpose of an Administrative Remedy Hearing is to allow each side of the anticipated case to engage in a face-to-face discussion in hopes an agreement can be reached without going to court. It really amounts to a pre-negotiation discussion. In some situations, a settlement is agreed on, and often a financial settlement agreement is the outcome of the meeting."

Attorney Woods—"The Board may not be interested in any such settlement; however, I think it would be wise for you to be aware of any possible demands which you may be exposed to—again, such as:

1. a complete reinstatement to former position
2. a buyout to include a full salary as stated in the current contract
3. a portion of the total amount specified as salary for the balance of the current contract
4. salary payment to the end of the current month
5. salary as of the current day of the month.

The hearing process and procedure is normally conducted by allowing each opposing attorney to devise a procedure which allows each side to make a presentation specifying their desired outcome from the proposed court appearance as well as defending any action which is a major concern to the opposing party."

Attorney Woods—"Do you have any questions concerning the Administrative Remedy Hearing process?"

Williams—"Then are we required to have the hearing?"

Attorney Woods—"If either party requests the hearing, then it is required."

Williams—"Suppose you approach them and determine if the hearing is necessary?"

Attorney Woods—"Very well. I will contact Duncan regarding the hearing."

At 7:10 a.m. the following day, Emmitt and Fry made a second visit to the high school practice field.

Emmitt—"Good!" We have no spectators."

Fry—"Emmitt, are you sure you want to go through with this? Remember what happened the last time when we came here to do this same thing?"

Emmitt—"Ellis, I have to know what I am capable of in the way of passing. Without my passing ability, I am a nobody as far as the coaching staff is concerned."

Fry—"But Emmitt, are we rushing our try-outs? Remember, Dr. Cowan said the recovery from your type of injury takes a long period of time."

Emmitt—"I am feeling much better, and the last time we were here, I threw for almost 62 plus yards. I want to make it close to 100 yards."

Fry—"Emmitt, I wish we would wait another week or ten days before we try it again."

Emmitt—"No, please work with me on this."

Fry—"Well, let's take our time in warming up."

They did take their time in warming up. Emmitt threw short passes of ten, fifteen, and twenty yards before extending the distance to forty and even fifty yards.

Fry—"Now, Emmitt, you are not short of breath after this workout so far, and your accuracy has improved over last time. Let's call it a day for now and come back on another day and try the long passes."

Emmitt—"I may not be short of breath this time, but you sure are! I have kept you running most of the morning. I'll try two more passes, and then we can go. O.K.?"

The first pass was for a distance of some 68 yards, and the second one was approaching 78 yards. Emmitt seemed satisfied, and they concluded the exercise.

The Administrative Remedy Hearing

Since there is no state law governing this procedure and conduct of such a hearing, the procedure will be bound by the administrative rules of the University. A retired member of the State Supreme Court, Raymond Stotzer, had agreed to preside at the hearing.

Judge Stotzer noted that both parties had agreed upon the date, time, and place for the hearing, and an informal atmosphere was to set the tone of the meeting. In addition, each party was to be given uninterrupted time to present their case. After both parties had made their presentations, a period of questioning would follow. The attorney representing each party would be fully in charge of the presentation to be made.

Judge Stotzer—"This meeting will come to order. This is an Administrative Remedy Hearing involving Bluefield University and Head Coach Will Havens. Mr. Havens' services to the University were terminated on XXXXXXXX by the Board of Regents. Mr. Havens is exercising his right of redress and is requesting that the Board of Regents review their decision to terminate his contract."

Judge Stotzer—"Mr. Mark Woods, as the attorney representing Bluefield University, you may proceed in presenting your initial reasons for terminating the services of Mr. Havens."

Attorney Woods—"The basis for the action taken regarding Coach Havens' termination was three-fold:

1. Intentionally presenting false information to the Board
2. Targeting a player
3. Deliberately placing a player in harm's way.

As to item number one, Coach Havens knowingly presented false information to the Board concerning two monetary payments for a total of $30,000. He claimed it was funds from the sale of his mother's estate when, in reality, it was a 'gift' from the parent of one of the current football squad members. We are prepared to show that the 'gift' payments influenced Havens' personnel decisions."

Attorney Woods—"As to item number two, targeting. Targeting takes place when a player is set up as the target for a certain activity. In this case, we feel that Emmitt Wilson, who was the passer for an offensive scrimmage team, was set up as a target for a defensive line plus certain secondary positions. Emmitt was the target for five defensive linemen plus two linebacks. Coach Havens was heard to yell at the defensive charger to 'TAKE HIM OUT OF THERE! HURT HIM!'" This is targeting, and it worked this time. Three linemen and one linebacker reached Emmitt at almost the same time resulting in a massive pile-up. Emmitt failed to get up and was sent to the hospital."

Attorney Woods—"As to item number three, Coach Havens deliberately placed a player in harm's way which resulted in a very serious injury with what seems to have incurred a lasting limitation to the individual's well-being. During a Wednesday afternoon scrimmage which concentrated on the defense rushing the offensive passer, the defense team composed of the Bluefield first-team had been unsuccessful in disrupting the passing of Emmitt Wilson. Coach Havens was heard to say, 'GET HIM OUT OF THERE! HURT HIM!' On the next play, the defense was successful in reaching the passer (Emmitt Wilson), and as a result, Emmitt was severely injured."

Attorney Woods—"We have additional detailed evidence to be presented at a later time. This concludes our initial presentation."

Judge Stotzer—"Mr. Duncan, are you now prepared to make your client's presentation?"

Attorney Duncan—"Yes, Judge Stotzer, we are ready. As to the charge that Coach Havens knowingly presented false information regarding two monetary payments for a total of $30,000, it is true. There is no evidence of a sale of such property. However, Coach Havens was not under oath at that time, which means that there is no penalty for such a statement."

Attorney Duncan—"Your Honor, I would like to have Coach Havens come forward to provide additional information concerning this phase of our presentation."

Attorney Duncan—"Coach Havens, please inform the Board of the details of your receiving the $30,000 gift."

Coach Havens—"It is true that I received a monetary gift of $30,000. The Board had asked for an explanation as to the source of the gift. I considered the source to be none of the Board's business—so my response was that the funds came from the sale of my mother's property."

Coach Havens continued—"I was surprised by the gift but was also aware that such a gift is legal. I was concerned that the morale of my coaching staff might be affected by such a gift and did not want to do anything to disrupt the pleasant relationship which existed in our athletic department."

Attorney Duncan—"What was the stipulation which was required if you accepted the gift."

Coach Havens—"None whatsoever. It was a thank you for my services rendered as a coach."

Attorney Duncan—"Are such gifts common in the coaching profession?"

Coach Havens—"I don't know! It is my first experience with a gift of any kind."

Attorney Duncan—"To further provide evidence regarding the gift, the individual who made the gift is here. I ask that he be allowed to make a statement concerning the gift. Would Mr. Marvin Gray please come forward? Mr. Gray, would you please state your name and the reason you have been asked to appear here today?"

Mr. Gray—"My name is Marvin Gray, and I am the individual who made the gift to Coach Havens."

Attorney Duncan—"How are you involved in the Bluefield football program?"

Mr. Gray—"I am the father of Jeff Gray who is a member of the current football squad."

Attorney Duncan—"Did you ask for anything in return for your gift?"

Mr. Gray—"Nothing at all!" My son's grandfather played professional football for eleven years. I had hoped that Jeff would be able to make the pros. I only asked if pro scouts ever expressed an interest in visiting the Bluefield program that I be informed. I am truly sorry for the grief I have caused Coach Havens. He is a fine coach and person, and I am honored to have my son play on a team he has coached."

Attorney Duncan—"Thank you, Mr. Gray. We appreciate receiving the information you have provided."

Attorney Duncan—"Coach Havens, please continue with your presentation."

Coach Havens—"As to number two—targeting a player. This is pure nonsense! It is absurd to even think a coach would target one of his own players. Emmitt was taking the position of a quarterback at what was to be our next opponent. Our entire scrimmage exercise was to disrupt the passer. This type of exercise is one used across the state in hundreds of football practice sessions during football season. Football players know there is a chance of injury every time there is a practice or a game. It is an accepted fact. I am truly sorry for the boy's injury, but it is a chance he took when he put on the football uniform. As for me supposedly yelling 'Take him out of there! Hurt him!'—it was during the heat of a practice. I did not say that! But during the excitement of a practice or a game, tempers often flare and people think they hear something. But I know what I said!"

Coach Havens continued—"As to the item number three—deliberately placing a player in harm's way. I suppose one could say that about all eleven players when a team takes to the field of play. There is always a chance of injury to any of the members of a team—whether it be offense or defense. As a coach, I placed each of the eleven members of the team in an assigned position. If any one of the eleven members is injured, have I placed them all in harm's way?"

Coach Havens again—"As a coach, it is my responsibility to assign players to a designated position. I am paid to do just that, but the player has some responsibility to try to execute his response to any called play to the best of his ability—which means to make every effort to avoid an injury of any kind. In this practice, the passer had been involved in seven straight pass plays and had avoided injury. On the next play, the eighth, he was unable to avoid injury. The defensive team was successful in carrying out their assigned task. The injury was not planned, and the severity of the event was unfortunate and is regretted by all concerned."

Attorney Duncan—"Judge Stotzer, this concludes our initial presentation."

Judge Stotzer—"Very well. Bluefield, you may proceed with the next phase of the hearing."

Attorney Woods—"Bluefield's investigation of Coach Havens' position concerning number one of our reasons for terminating his contract is that lying is a common practice so long as you are not under oath. I hope that young men who make up our football team do not accept this as common practice for adults. I certainly do not believe that bearing false witness is an accepted practice in the business world as well as in common everyday dealings."

Attorney Woods continues—"As to item two—targeting a player—the fact that no 'red practice jacket' was in use during such a concentrated practice with eleven defensive positions going after a single individual (the passer) indicates not only targeting but CONCENTRATED targeting."

Attorney Woods—"As to deliberately placing a player in harm's way, Coach Havens was heard to say 'Take him out of there! Hurt him!' To this statement the coach says he knows what he said. So do at least a dozen individuals who were at the practice session."

Attorney Woods continues—"It is true that a coach has the assignment of placing players in a position of his own choice. But it is also true that he is expected to use his professional judgment in exercising every safety precaution in so doing. Every action taken at this practice session indicates that this was not done."

Attorney Woods—"Judge Stotzer, this concludes our presentation."

Judge Stotzer—"Very well. Are there any other parties wishing to make comments?"

Judge Stotzer—"The chair recognizes Coach Havens."

Coach Havens—"Thank you, judge. My question is directed to the Board of Regents. I respectfully request the Board to reconsider my termination. I have given what I think has been outstanding service to the University during my four years as head coach. The situation we are discussing today is the only blemish on my record. I have learned from this chain of events and will certainly never make anything like the same mistake again."

Judge Stotzer—"Thank you. Are there any other questions?"

Chairman Peebles—"Judge, the Board of Regents does not have a question. However, we would like to make a statement which represents the unanimous thinking of the members of the Board of Regents."

Judge Stotzer—"Very well. Proceed."

Chairman Peebles—"Coach Havens, any coach that would do what you have done to Emmitt Wilson does not need to be around young athletes. I hope you take a long look at what you caused to be done to this boy. All indications point to the fact that the boy had a potential with untold boundaries of success. He has been robbed of this possible success."

Silence gripped the room.

Judge Stotzer—"Are there any other questions or statements at this time? There being none, this hearing is now adjourned."

As the hearing broke up, there were a few exchanges of dialogues—for one thing, Havens said to no one in particular: "I'll see you people in court!"

Chairman Peebles—"We will look forward to the exchange of opinions."

As a follow-up after the hearing, the Board of Regents assembled for a brief meeting.

Attorney Woods—"The next several weeks will involve our preparation for the court action. I will meet from time to time with witnesses I plan to call and also with individuals from the Board. As I build our defense, I will keep members of the Board informed. This may involve regular meetings or emails or phone conversations."

Chairman Peebles—"Mark, what period of time are we talking about? I would like to move this procedure along as fast as possible."

Attorney Woods—"It is difficult to even estimate. I would imagine several weeks. This will be determined by when we can get on the courts' and the judges' court calendars. But I feel as you do—it will be to our advantage to move forward quickly. However, keep in mind that I am sure Havens would want a quick calendar date since he is unemployed at this time."

Spurlock—"What can the members of the Board do during the meantime?"

Attorney Woods—"Just respond to me as quickly as you can when I request information or action."

Life is what happens to you when you're busy making other plans.

John Lennon

CHAPTER FOURTEEN

WAYWARD WINDS OF A PROFESSION

CHAPTER FOURTEEN

1. Administrative Procedures Set in Motion
2. Emmitt's Third Visit to the Practice Field
3. Two News Releases by Bluefield University
4. Internment
5. Herb Gormley's Sports Column

WAYWARD WINDS OF A PROFESSION

Attorney Woods—"Since the Board of Regents has initiated the termination process for head Coach Havens, a series of administrative procedures should be set in motion. For example:

*Would the university request the case be heard in State Court or Federal Court?

*Make an analysis of what had led to the current situation

*Is the termination based on

1. Error in judgement

2. Breach of contract

3. Targeting one of his own players

4. Unsatisfactory behavior of an individual

5. Placing a player in harm's way.

Consider again possible settlement of the case before going to trial such as:

1. Reinstatement to former position
2. A buyout to include full salary as stated in the contract
3. A portion of the total amount specified as salary for the balance of the current contract
4. No buy out of any kind.

I realize the Board of Regents has stated that they have no interest in any type of settlement, but such issues will be brought to the table for discussion."

Attorney Woods—"The Board of Regents needs to be involved in a discussion of the following items:

1. Time involved in such a case
2. Projected cost
3. Review of the University's Personnel Manual
4. Discussion of the details and interpretation of the University Employee Rights Manual.

Once the Board has decided on their reaction to possible settlement questions, I will be able to proceed with our defense strategy."

Four days after their second visit to the practice field, Emmitt and Fry made a third visit.

Emmitt—"O.K. Ellis, we are going to put things to the test today. It should give us an indicator of what the future holds for this old boy from Sparta High School."

Fry—"Once we see what progress we have made to date, then we can move at a slower pace in getting you back to your old self."

They took their time in the warm-up exercises, starting off with short passes of 10, 20, and 30 yards. Then they moved into passes of 40 and 50 yards.

Emmitt—"The arm feels pretty good today. It has not gotten that numb feeling that I experienced the last time we were here."

Fry—"Good! That is progress!"

They took their time because Ellis was getting a real workout, running all the pass routes with little time in between passes.

Emmitt—"O.K., let's take a fifteen-minute break, then we are going to try the long passes."

Fry—"That sounds good, but I need more than a 10-minute break between each of your long passes. Let's try a 15-minute break."

Emmitt—"Sounds like a winner! I am ready whenever you are."

The first long pass was well over 80 yards, and the second pass was 93 yards.

After another break, Emmitt said, "O.K., let's try one more, and then we will call it a day!"

Fry took off on what would be the route of the passing pattern for the long pass. Emmitt took his passing stance and at the appropriate distance started his long pass motion, but as his arm came forward over his shoulder, he collapsed and fell to the ground. Fry broke off the pass route and raced back to Emmitt's prone body on the ground. Emmitt seemed to be unconscious and was bleeding from his mouth and eyes.

An ambulance was called, but Emmitt died on the way to the hospital.

The athletic department together with the Bluefield University campus was in disarray following the news of the death of Emmitt Wilson. Many people thought the possibility of such an event had passed, and their attention had turned to the progress of an extended recovery which was uppermost in the minds of those who were mindful of casual observations.

While packing Emmitt's belongings in his room, the following note was found in the drawer of his desk. It was at first thought that it might be a suicide note. However, as it turned out, Emmitt had made statements to Fry and Mobley which proved otherwise. He had indicated in conversations that due to the seriousness of his accident, he realized that something of this nature might happen and, if it did, he wanted to leave a message to his parents. He referred to it as a "just in case" note. Therefore, based on the evidence available, neither the doctors nor the legal officials considered the letter to be a suicide note.

Dear Mom and Dad,

You have been such wonderful parents only now do I realize how much you have sacrificed for me to have the wonderful life I enjoyed as a child, a teenager and a college student.

The athletic ability that I worked so hard to develope and perfect was cut short before it could produce, and I cannot get over the crushing disappointment.

My love will always be with you.

Much love,
Emmitt

The following day, the Bluefield University issued the following news release:

While participating in a football workout yesterday afternoon, Emmitt Wilson collapsed and died on the way to the hospital. Emmitt was a quarterback on the Bluefield University football team. He was classified as a junior and had been a member of the football squad since his freshman year.

No details have been released concerning the internment of Emmitt Wilson at this time.

INTERNMENT

Within a few hours after Emmitt's death, the media zeroed in on the story of Emmitt's attendance at Bluefield University. The media included newspapers, radio stations, and television channels. The news coverage went back to his high school days when he had played six-man football on to the time he entered Bluefield University without a scholarship but paid his way by working his way through college as a custodian in one of the University buildings.

The coverage included mention of his position on the playing chart as a third-team quarterback and his limited playing time of only thirty-seven minutes in the first seven games of the current season. It went on to site his passing accomplishments of three one-hundred-yard pass completions as well as two eighty-three-yard completions and numerous fifty- and sixty-yard passes. However, the coverage stressed that he was never listed as more than a third-string quarterback.

Coach Havens' having received the thirty-thousand-dollar gift also received much press, although it never named the parent or the player involved. Most of the coaches and players refused to be interviewed or even make comments regarding this incident. Paramount in much of the news coverage was the question of why such a talented individual was so limited in playing time. It has been said that $30,000 really bought out Emmitt's football career and reminds one of the Bible story when Judas betrayed Christ for 30 pieces of silver.

Emmitt's internment was held at a country church in Coryell County in an out-of-the-way cemetery with a typical open-air tabernacle. It was the same place of worship he had attended while growing up on the family ranch. Even though this was an out-of-the-way cemetery and almost one hundred miles from the Bluefield campus, some three hundred people attended the services.

COACH HAVENS

Two days following the funeral of Emmitt Wilson, Bluefield University issued the following news release:

The Bluefield University is saddened to inform the public of the death of Coach Will Havens. Mr. Havens was serving as head coach of the University's football program at the time of his death. He was in his fifth year of service to the University and had come to Bluefield University from Mississippi Tech. Under his leadership, Bluefield University had won the conference championship for the past two years.

No details have been released concerning the internment of Will Havens at this time.

THE NATIONAL NEWS SERVICE
SPORTS REVIEW
by
HERB GORMLEY

He never made an all-American team.

He never made the all-conference team.

He never even made the second Bluefield University team.

Although I firmly believe he is destined to go into the conference history books as one of the outstanding all-time passers of the modern football era.

I had a meeting with Wilson several days before his accident. I was much impressed with his friendliness and personality. For his young age, he had made a deep study of the game of football. The routine he had developed for the long pass was fascinating. He must have had some type of self-initiated exercise program most of his teenage years which built for him an exceptionally strong upper body with an emphasis on the arms.

I asked him about his ability to throw the extra-long pass. He was unable to explain what he termed the flip-motion which he used as he released each long pass delivery although he stated that he used it each time he released the long pass.

To set up a long pass play, he said it takes extra timing as the receiver must be able to get within eighty to ninety yards down the field before the pass is released. According to Wilson's scheme of operations, he must have at least four seconds to move from under the center to four or nine yards behind the line of scrimmage with an additional two seconds to select and set up his passing stance which allows up to three seconds for the ball to be in flight to the receiver. If these conditions are not achievable, the long pass is aborted.

I never understood the coaching staff's refusal to place any value on his six-man football experience. To me, six-man football is an exhausting activity. With the wide-open type of offense, both offensive and defensive players are running most of the playing time. Open field blocking and tackling constitute most of the individual position requirements. Wilson played six-man football for Sparta High School—one of the most successful six-man teams in the entire state. Yet in analyzing his background, the staff said his six-man experience was not of the caliber of our current quarterback's experience. I always thought it was an insult to him when the head coach referred to Wilson as 'what's his name.' Incidentally, that happened at the game when he threw his first one-hundred-yard pass completion which won the game for his team.

I realize that Bluefield University had two other quarterbacks —one of which had led the team to winning seasons the last two years; however, the concept of team athletics is to select the most talented individual for each position thereby being able to present the best team to represent a school or university. I know the coach has the responsibility to make these decisions; however, in this case, ulterior motives may have played a part in the position selection process.

Emmitt repeatedly demonstrated passing skills I had never seen before. My purpose in dwelling on this subject is that I think the football sports history has been robbed of observing an outstanding talent which should have been displayed for years to come. Emmitt Wilson was denied his future greatness by an ill-advised afternoon practice.

I have been involved in this scenario since the day after the beginning of practice. I have been a spectator at practice sessions; I have attended Bluefield games; I have had extensive talks with coaches and players; and I have been a sports reporter for a major newspaper for sixteen years. All of this is to say as to coaching and player demands of the game of football, I am a first-hand witness. Emmitt Wilson demonstrated passing skills far above anything ever displayed during my tenure as a sports reporter.

With the passing of Emmitt Wilson—who possessed a fantastic talent— Coach Havens, the three assistant coaches who have changed professions, as well as the two linemen who tackled Wilson in the scrimmage and who have now dropped out of any football program, and after analyzing the other events involving the major characters of these last several weeks, my concluding comment is

THERE WERE NO SURVIVORS.

www.ingramcontent.com/pod-product-compliance
Lightning Source LLC
LaVergne TN
LVHW011929070526
838202LV00054B/4550